"I only have eyes for one woman here."

"Oh? And who would that be?"

"You."

A shiver washed over her, despite herself. "Cole, don't."

His expression sobered. "There's unfinished business between us, Cassie. You know there is. I think it's about time we dealt with it."

"I can't think about that now. I can't think about you," she said fiercely, scrambling to her feet.

"I'll still be here when you get back," he reminded her. "And nothing will have changed."

Cassie didn't care. She needed time to figure out why Cole could still get to her.

"You do whatever you want to do," she told him. "You always have."

That said, she fled. Thinking about the man couldn't get her into that much trouble.

Being with him could be disastrous.

Get caught reading Silhouette.

Dear Reader,

May marks the celebration of "Get Caught Reading," a national campaign the Association of American Publishers created to promote the sheer joy of reading. "Get Caught Reading" may be a phrase that's familiar to you, but if not, we hope you'll familiarize yourself with it by picking up the wonderful selections that Silhouette Special Edition has to offer....

Former NASA engineer Laurie Paige says that when she was young, she checked out *The Little Engine That Could* from the library fifty times. "I read it every week," Laurie recalls. "I was so astounded that the library would lend books to me for free. I've been an avid reader ever since." Though Laurie Paige hasn't checked out her favorite childhood storybook for a while, she now participates in several local literacy fund-raisers and reads to young children in her community. Laurie is also a prolific writer, with nearly forty published Silhouette titles, including this month's *Something To Talk About*.

Don't miss the fun when a once-burned rancher discovers that the vivacious amnesiac he's helping turns out to be the missing Stockwell heiress in Jackie Merritt's *The Cattleman and the Virgin Heiress*. And be sure to catch all of THE CALAMITY JANES, five friends sharing the struggles and celebrations of life, starting with *Do You Take This Rebel?* by Sherryl Woods. And what happens when Willa and Zach learn they both inherited the same ranch? Find out in *The Ties That Bind* by Ginna Gray. Be sure to see who will finish first in Patricia Hagan's *Race to the Altar*. And Judith Lyons pens a highly emotional tale with *Lt. Kent: Lone Wolf*.

So this May, make time for books. Remember how fun it is to browse a bookstore, hold a book in your hands and discover new worlds on the printed page.

Best,

Karen Taylor Richman
Senior Editor

Please address questions and book requests to:
Silhouette Reader Service
U.S.: 3010 Walden Ave., P.O. Box 1325, Buffalo, NY 14269
Canadian: P.O. Box 609, Fort Erie, Ont. L2A 5X3

Sherryl Woods

DO YOU TAKE THIS REBEL?

Silhouette

SPECIAL EDITION™

Published by Silhouette Books

America's Publisher of Contemporary Romance

For the Potomac Sunrise gang—Carolyn, Jim and
Diane—for helping me to keep my stories on track and
for sharing their own fabulous writing with me. And a
special thanks to Carolyn, who rose to the challenge
and came up with the title for *The Calamity Janes*.

 SILHOUETTE BOOKS

ISBN 0-373-24394-4

DO YOU TAKE THIS REBEL?

Copyright © 2001 by Sherryl Woods

Visit Silhouette at www.eHarlequin.com

Printed in U.S.A.

Books by Sherryl Woods

Silhouette Special Edition

Safe Harbor #425
Never Let Go #446
Edge of Forever #484
In Too Deep #522
Miss Liz's Passion #573
Tea and Destiny #595
My Dearest Cal #669
Joshua and the Cowgirl #713
*Love #769
*Honor #775
*Cherish #781
*Kate's Vow #823
*A Daring Vow #855
*A Vow To Love #885
The Parson's Waiting #907
One Step Away #927
Riley's Sleeping Beauty #961
Finally a Bride #987
‡*A Christmas Blessing* #1001
‡*Natural Born Daddy* #1007
‡*The Cowboy and His Baby* #1009

‡*The Rancher and His Unexpected
    Daughter* #1016
**A Ranch for Sara #1083
***Ashley's Rebel* #1087
***Danielle's Daddy Factor* #1094
††*The Littlest Angel* #1142
††*Natural Born Trouble* #1156
††*Unexpected Mommy* #1171
††*The Cowgirl and the
    Unexpected Wedding* #1208
††*Natural Born Lawman* #1216
††*The Cowboy and His Wayward
    Bride* #1234
††*Suddenly, Annie's Father* #1268
◊*The Cowboy and the New Year's
    Baby* #1291
◊*Dylan and the Baby Doctor* #1309
◊*The Pint-Sized Secret* #1333
◊*Marrying a Delacourt* #1352
◊*The Delacourt Scandal* #1363
A Love Beyond Words #1382
§*Do You Take This Rebel* #1394

Silhouette Desire

Not at Eight, Darling #309
Yesterday's Love #329
Come Fly with Me #345
A Gift of Love #375
Can't Say No #431
Heartland #472
One Touch of Moondust #521
Next Time... Forever #601
Fever Pitch #620
Dream Mender #708

Silhouette Books

Silhouette Summer Sizzlers 1990
"A Bridge to Dreams"

Maternity Leave 1998
"The Paternity Test"

††*The Unclaimed Baby*

*Vows
‡And Baby Makes Three
**The Bridal Path
††And Baby Makes Three:
    The Next Generation
◊And Baby Makes Three:
    The Delacourts of Texas
§The Calamity Janes

SHERRYL WOODS

has written more than seventy-five romances and mysteries in the past twenty years. And because she loves to talk to real people once in a while, she also operates her own bookstore, Potomac Sunrise, in Colonial Beach, VA, where readers from around the country stop by to discuss her favorite topic—books. If you can't visit Sherryl at her store, then be sure to drop her a note at P.O. Box 490326, Key Biscayne, FL 33149.

Winding River High School
Class of '91

Welcome Home — Ten Years Later
Do You Remember the Way We Were?

Cassie Collins — Ringleader of the Calamity Janes. Elected most likely to land in jail. Best known for painting the town water tower a shocking pink and for making the entire faculty regret choosing teaching as a profession. Class record for detentions.

Karen (Phipps) Hanson — Better known as The Dreamer. Elected most likely to see the world. Member of the 4-H club, the Spanish and French clubs, and first-place winner at the county fair in the greased pig contest.

Gina Petrillo — Tastiest girl in the class. Elected most popular because nobody in town bakes a better double chocolate brownie. Member of the Future Homemakers of America. Winner of three blue ribbons in the pie-baking contest and four in the cake-baking contest at the county fair.

Emma Rogers — That girl can swing...a bat, that is. Elected most likely to be the first female on the New York Yankees. Member of the Debate Club, the Honor Society and president of the senior class.

Lauren Winters — The girl with all the answers, otherwise known as the one you'd most like to be seated next to during an exam. Elected most likely to succeed. Class valedictorian. Member of the Honor Society, County Fair Junior Rodeo Queen and star of the junior and senior class plays.

Prologue

The thick white envelope had all the formality of a wedding invitation. Cassie weighed it in her hands, her gaze locked on the postmark—Winding River, Wyoming. Her hometown. A place she sometimes longed for in the dark of night when she could hear her heart instead of her common sense, when hope outdistanced regrets.

Face facts, she told herself sternly. She didn't belong there anymore. The greatest gift she'd ever given to her mother was her having left town. Her high school friends—the Calamity Janes, they'd called themselves, in honor of their penchant for broken hearts and trouble—were all scattered now. The man she'd once loved with everything in her... Well, who knew where he was? More than likely he was back in Winding River, running the ranch that would be his legacy from his powerful, domineering father. She hadn't asked, because to do so would be an admission that he still mattered, even after he'd betrayed her, leaving her alone and pregnant.

Still, she couldn't seem to help the stirring of anticipation that she felt as she ran her fingers over the fancy calligraphy and wondered what was inside. Was one of her best friends getting married? Was it a baby announcement? Whatever it was, it was bound to evoke a lot of old memories.

Finally, reluctantly, she broke the seal and pulled out the thick sheaf of pages inside. Right on top, written in more of that intricate calligraphy, was the explanation: a ten-year high school reunion, scheduled for two months away at the beginning of July. The additional pages described all of the activities planned—a dance, a picnic, a tour of the new addition to the school. There would be lots of time for reminiscing. It would all be capped off by the town's annual parade and fireworks on the Fourth of July.

Her first thought was of the Calamity Janes. Would they all be there? Would Gina come back from New York, where she was running a fancy Italian restaurant? Would Emma leave Denver and the fast track she was on at her prestigious law firm? And even though she was less than a hundred miles away, would Karen be able to get away from her ranch and its never-ending, back-breaking chores? Then, of course, there was Lauren, the studious one, who'd stunned them all by becoming one of Hollywood's top box-office stars. Would she come back to a small town in Wyoming for something as ordinary as a class reunion?

Just the possibility of seeing them all was enough to bring a lump to Cassie's throat and a tear to her eyes. Oh, how she had missed them. They were as different as night and day. Their lives had taken wildly divergent paths, but somehow they had always managed to stay in touch, to stay as close as sisters despite the infrequent contact. They had rejoiced over the four marriages among them, over the births of children, over career triumphs. And they had cried over Lauren's two divorces and Emma's one.

Cassie would give anything to see them, but it was out of the question. The timing, the cost...it just wouldn't work.

"Mom, are you crying?"

Cassie cast a startled look at her son, whose brow was puckered by a frown. "Of course not," she said, swiping away the telltale dampness on her cheek. "Must have gotten something in my eye."

Jake peered at her skeptically, but then his attention was caught by the papers she was holding. "What are those?" he asked, trying to get a look.

Cassie held them out of his reach. "Just some stuff from Winding River," she said.

"From Grandma?" he asked, his eyes lighting up.

Despite her mood, Cassie grinned. Her mother, with whom she'd always been at odds over one thing or another, was her son's favorite person, mainly because she spoiled him outrageously on her infrequent visits. She also had a habit of tucking money for Jake into her dutiful, weekly letters to Cassie. And for his ninth birthday, a few months back, she had sent him a check. There'd been no mistaking how grownup he'd felt when he'd taken it into the bank to cash it.

"No, it's not from Grandma," she said. "It's from my old school."

"How come?"

"They're having a reunion this summer and I'm invited."

His expression brightened. "Are we gonna go? That would be so awesome. We hardly ever go to see Grandma. I was just a baby last time."

Not a baby, she thought. He'd been five, but to him it must seem like forever. She'd never had the heart to tell him that the trips were so infrequent because his beloved grandmother liked it that way. Not that she'd ever discouraged Cassie from coming home, but she certainly hadn't encouraged it. She'd always seemed more comfortable coming to visit them, far away from those judgmental stares of her friends and neighbors. As dearly as Edna Collins loved Jake, his illegitimacy grated on her moral values. At least she placed the blame for that where it belonged—with Cassie. She had never held it against Jake.

"I doubt it, sweetie. I probably won't be able to get time off from work."

Jake's face took on an increasingly familiar mutinous look. "I'll bet Earlene would let you go if you asked."

"I can't ask," she said flatly. "It's the middle of the tourist season. The restaurant is always busy in summer. You know that. That's when I make the best tips. We need the money from every single weekend to make it through the slow winter months."

She tried never to say much about their precarious financial status because she figured a nine-year-old didn't need to have that burden weighing on him. But she also wanted Jake to be realistic about what they could and couldn't afford. A trip to Winding River, no matter how badly either of them might want to make it, wasn't in the cards. It was the lost wages, not the cost of the drive itself, that kept her from agreeing.

"I could help," he said. "Earlene will pay me to bus tables when it's busy."

"I'm sorry, kiddo. I don't think so."

"But, Mom—"

"I said no, Jake, and that's the end of it." To emphasize the point, she tore up the invitation and tossed it in the trash.

Later that night, regretting the impulsive gesture, she went back to get the pieces, but they were gone. Jake had retrieved them, no doubt, though she couldn't imagine why. Of course, Winding River didn't mean the same thing to him as it did to her—mistakes, regrets and, if she was being totally honest, a few very precious, though painful, memories.

Her son didn't understand any of that. He knew only that his grandmother was there, the sole family he had, other than his mom. If Cassie had had any idea just how badly he missed Edna or just how far he would go for the chance to see her again, she would have burned that invitation without ever having opened it.

By the time she found out, Jake was in more trouble than she'd ever imagined getting into, and her life was about to take one of those calamitous turns she and her friends were famous for.

Chapter One

Nine-year-old Jake Collins didn't exactly look like a big-time criminal. In fact, Cassie thought her son looked an awful lot like a scared little boy as he sat across the desk from the sheriff, sneaker-clad feet swinging a good six inches off the floor, his glasses sliding down his freckled nose. When he pushed them up, she could see the tears in his blue eyes magnified by the thick lenses. It was hard to feel sorry for him, though, when he was the reason for the twisting knot in her stomach and for the uncharacteristically stern look on the sheriff's face.

"What you've done is very serious," Sheriff Joshua Cartwright said. "You understand that, don't you?"

Jake's head bobbed. "Yes, sir," he whispered.

"It's stealing," the sheriff added.

Jake's chin rose indignantly. "I didn't steal nothing from those people."

"You took their money and you didn't send them the toys you promised," Joshua said. "You made a deal and you didn't keep your end of it. That's the same as stealing."

Cassie knew that the only reason the sheriff wasn't being even harder on Jake was because of her boss. Earlene ran the diner where Cassie worked, and Joshua had been courting the woman for the past six months, ever since Earlene had worked up the courage to toss out her drunken, sleazebag husband. The sheriff spent a lot of time at the diner and knew that Earlene was as protective as a mother hen where Cassie and Jake were concerned.

In fact, even now Earlene was hovering outside waiting to learn what had possessed Joshua to haul her favorite little boy down to his office. If she didn't like the answer, Cassie had no doubt there would be hell for the sheriff to pay.

"How bad is it?" Cassie asked, dreading the answer. She didn't have much in the way of savings at this time of year with the summer tourist season just starting. The total in her bank account was a few hundred dollars at most. That paltry sum was all that stood between them and financial disaster.

"Two thousand, two hundred and fifty dollars, plus some change," the sheriff said, reading the total from a report in front of him.

Cassie gasped at the amount. "There has to be some mistake. Who in heaven's name would send that much money to a boy they don't even know?" she demanded.

"Not just one person. Dozens of them. They all bid on auctions that Jake put up on the Internet. When the time came to send them the items, he didn't."

Cassie was flabbergasted. The Internet was something she had absolutely no experience with. How on earth could her son know enough to use it to con people?

"I started getting calls last week from people claiming that a person in town was running a scam," the sheriff continued. He shook his head. "When the first person gave me the name, I have to tell you, I almost fell off my chair. Just like you, I thought it had to be some mistake. When the calls kept coming, I couldn't ignore it. I figured there had to be some truth to it. I checked down at the post office, and Louella confirmed that Jake had been cashing a lot of money orders. It didn't occur to her to question why a kid his age was getting so much mail, all of it with money orders."

Ignoring the dull ache in her chest, Cassie faced her son. "Then it's true? You did do this?"

Defiance flashed briefly in his eyes, but then he lowered his head and whispered, "Yes, ma'am."

Cassie stared at him. Jake was a smart kid. She knew that. She also understood that his troublemaking behavior was a bid for attention, just as hers had been years ago. But this took the occasional brawl at school or shoplifting a pack of gum to a whole new level. His behavior had gotten worse since she had refused to consider going to Winding River so he could spend some time with his grandmother.

"How did you even get access to the Internet?" she asked him. "We don't have a computer."

"The school does," he said defensively. "I get extra credit for using it."

"Somehow I doubt they'd give a lot of credit for running cons on some auction site," the sheriff said dryly. He glanced at Cassie. "Unfortunately, there's nothing to keep a kid from putting something up for sale. Most sites rely on feedback from customers to keep the sellers honest. As I understand it, most of Jake's auctions ran back-to-back within a day or two of each other, so by the time there was negative feedback, it was too late. He had the money. The auction site manager called this morning, following up on the complaints they had received, and looking for their cut, as well."

"What kind of toys were you promising these people, Jake?" Cassie asked, still struggling to grasp the idea that strangers had actually sent her son over two thousand dollars. That was more than she earned in tips in several months.

"Just some stuff," Jake mumbled.

"Baseball cards, Pokémon cards, rare Beanie Babies," the sheriff said, reading from that same report. "Looks like he'd been watching the site. He knew exactly what items to list for sale, which ones would bring top dollar from kids and collectors."

"And where is this money?" Cassie asked, imagining it squandered on who knew what.

"I've been saving it," Jake explained, his studious little face suddenly intense. "For something real important."

"Saving it?" she repeated, thinking of the little metal box that contained his most treasured possessions and those dollars that his grandmother sent. Had he been socking away that much cash in there? All of his friends knew about that box. Any one of them could steal the contents.

"Where?" she asked, praying he'd put it someplace more secure.

"In my box," he said, confirming her worst fears.

"Oh, Jake."

"It's safe," he insisted. "I hid it where nobody would ever find it."

There was a dull throbbing behind Cassie's eyes. She resisted the temptation to rub her temples, resisted even harder the desire to cry.

"But why would you do something like this?" she asked, still at a loss. "You had to know it was wrong. I just don't understand. Why did you need so much money? Were you hoping to buy your own computer?"

He shook his head. "I did it for you, Mom."

"Me?" she said, aghast. "Why?"

"So we could go back home for your reunion and maybe stay there for a really long time. I know you want to, even though you said you didn't." He regarded her with another touch of defiance. "Besides, I miss Grandma."

"Oh, baby, I know you do," Cassie said with a sigh. "So do I, but this…this was wrong. The sheriff is right. It was stealing."

"It's not like I took a whole lot from anybody," he insisted stubbornly. "They just paid for some dumb old cards and toys. They probably would have lost 'em, anyway."

"That's not the point," she said impatiently. "They paid you for them. You have to send every penny of the money back, unless you have the toys to make things right."

She figured that was highly unlikely, since Jake spent his allowance on books, not toys. She met the sheriff's gaze. "You have a list of all the people involved?"

"Right here. As far as I know, it's complete."

"If Jake sends the money back and writes a note of

apology to each one, will that take care of everything?''

''I imagine most of the people will be willing to drop any charges once they get their money back and hear the whole story,'' he said. ''I think a lot of them felt pretty foolish when they realized they were dealing with a third-grader.''

''Yeah, well, Jake is obviously nine going on thirty,'' Cassie said. At this rate he'd be running real estate scams by ten and stock market cons by his teens.

This was not the first time she had faced the fact that she was in way over her head when it came to raising her son. Every single mom struggled. In all likelihood, every single mom had doubts about her ability to teach right and wrong. Cassie had accepted that it wouldn't be easy when she'd made the decision to raise Jake on her own with no family at all nearby to help out.

And it should have been okay. They might never be rich, but Jake was loved. She had a steady job. Their basic needs were met. There were plenty of positive influences in his life.

Maybe if Jake had been an average little kid, everything would have been just fine, but he had his father's brilliance and her penchant for mischief. It was clearly a dangerous combination.

''If you'll give me that list of names, Jake will write the notes tonight. We'll be back in the morning with those and the money,'' she said grimly.

''But, Mom,'' Jake began. One look at Cassie's face and the protest died on his lips. His expression turned sullen.

''Jake, could you wait outside with Earlene for just a minute?'' the sheriff said. ''I'd like to speak to your mother.''

Jake slid out of the chair and, with one last backward glance, left the room. When he'd gone, Joshua faced Cassie, eyes twinkling.

"That boy of yours is a handful," he said.

"No kidding."

"You ever think about getting together with his daddy? Seems to me like he could use a man's influence."

"Not a chance," Cassie said fiercely.

Cole Davis might be the smartest, sexiest man she'd ever met. He might be the son of Winding River's biggest rancher. But she wouldn't marry him if he were the last chance she had to escape the fires of hell. He'd sweet-talked her into his bed when she was eighteen and he was twenty, but once that mission had been accomplished, she hadn't set eyes on him again. He'd gone back to college without so much as a goodbye.

When she'd discovered she was pregnant, she was too proud to try to track Cole down and plead for help. She'd left town, her reputation in tatters, determined to build a decent life for herself and her baby someplace where people weren't always expecting the worst of her.

Not that she hadn't given them cause to think poorly of her. She'd been rebellious from the moment she'd discovered that breaking the rules was a whole lot more fun than following them. She'd given her mother fits from the time she'd been a two-year-old whose favorite word was no, right on through her teens when she hadn't said no nearly enough.

If there was trouble in town, Cassie was the first person everyone looked to as ringleader. Her pregnancy hadn't surprised a single soul. Rather than endure the knowing looks and clucking remarks, rather than ask her mother to do the same, she'd simply fled, stopping in the first town where she'd spotted a Help Wanted sign in a diner window.

In the years since, she had made only rare trips back to visit her mother, and she'd never once asked about Cole or his family. If her mother suspected who Jake's father was, she'd never admitted it. The topic was off-limits to this day. Jake was Cassie's alone. Most of the time she was justifiably proud of the job she'd done raising him. She resented Joshua's implication that she wasn't up to the task on her own.

"Are you saying Jake wouldn't have done this if his father had been around?" she asked, an edge to her voice. "What could he have done that I haven't? I've taught Jake that it's wrong to steal. The message has been reinforced in Sunday school. And, believe me, he will be punished for this. He may well be grounded till he's twenty-one."

Joshua held up his hand. "I wasn't criticizing you. Kids get into trouble even with the best parents around, but with boys especially, they need a solid male role model."

Cassie didn't especially want her son following in Cole Davis's footsteps. There had to be better role models around. One was sitting right in front of her.

"He has you, Joshua," she pointed out. "Since you've been coming around the diner, he's spent a lot of time with you. He looks up to you. If anyone represents authority and law and order, you do. Did that help?"

"Point taken." He regarded her with concern. "Are you going to take that trip Jake was talking about? Obviously, it's something that he really cares about."

"I don't see how we can."

"If it's a matter of money, the way the boy said, it could be worked out," he said. "Earlene and I—"

"I'm not taking money from you," she said fiercely. "Or from Earlene. She's done enough for me."

"I think you should consider it," Joshua said slowly. His expression turned uneasy. "Look, Earlene would have my hide if she knew I was suggesting this, but I think you might want to give some thought to staying in Winding River when you do go back there." He said it as if their going was a done deal despite her expressed reluctance.

Cassie stared at him in shock. "Are you throwing us out of town?"

Joshua chuckled. "Nothing that dramatic. I was just thinking that it might be good for Jake to have more family around, more people to look out for him, lend a little extra stability to his life. It would be a help to you and maybe keep him out of mischief. This latest escapade can't be dismissed as easily as some of the others. Sometimes even kids need a fresh start. I've heard you tell Earlene yourself that he gives his teachers fits at school. Maybe a whole new environment where no one's expecting the worst would help him settle down. Better to get him in hand now than when he hits his teens and the trouble can get a whole lot more serious."

"I know," Cassie said, defeated. Nobody knew better than she did about fresh starts and living down past mistakes. Even so, it wasn't as easy as Joshua made it sound. She didn't bother to explain that her mother was all the family they'd have in Winding River and that friends there were few and far between. She had a stronger support system right here. Unfortunately, Joshua clearly didn't want to hear that.

"I'll think about it," she said eventually. "I promise."

But going home for a few days for a class reunion was one thing. Going back to live in the same town where Cole Davis and his father ruled was quite another.

Unfortunately, though, it sounded as if circumstances—and the well-intentioned sheriff—might not be giving her much choice.

"Blast it all, boy, I ain't getting any younger," Frank Davis grumbled over the eggs, ham and grits that were likely to do him in. "Who's going to run this ranch when I die?"

Cole put down his fork and sighed. He and his father had had this same discussion at least a thousand times in the past eight years.

"I thought that was why I was here," Cole said. "So you could go to your eternal rest knowing that the ranch was still in Davis hands."

His father waved off the comment. "Your heart's not in this place. I might as well admit it. It could fall down around us for all the attention you pay it. You spend half the night locked away in that office of yours with all that fancy computer equipment. For the life of me I can't figure what's so all-fired fascinating about staring at a screen with a bunch of gobbledy-gook on it."

"Last year that gobbledy-gook earned three times as much as this ranch," Cole pointed out, knowing even as he spoke that his father wouldn't be impressed. If it didn't have to do with cattle or land, Frank Davis didn't trust it. Cole had given up expecting his father to be proud of his accomplishments in the high-tech world.

He got higher praise when he negotiated top dollar for their cattle at market.

"All I have to say is, if I'd known then what I know now, I wouldn't have been so quick to break up you and that Collins girl. Maybe you'd have been settled down by now. Maybe you would have a little respect for this ranch your great-grandfather started."

Cole was not about to head off down that particular path. Any discussion of Cassie was doomed. He remembered all too clearly what had happened the minute his father had learned that the two of them were getting close. He had packed up Cole's things and shipped him off to school weeks before the start of his junior year.

To his everlasting regret, there hadn't been a thing Cole could do about it. At that point he'd wanted his college diploma too much to risk his father's wrath. That diploma had been his ticket away from ranching. He'd sent a note to Cassie explaining and begging for her understanding. Her reply had been curt. She'd told him it didn't matter, that he could do whatever suited him. She intended to get on with her life.

Ironically, the ink had barely been dry on his diploma when his father had suffered a heart attack and pleaded with him to return home. Now here he was, spending his days running the ranch he hated and his nights working on the computer programming he loved. It wasn't as awful as it could have been. The reality was he could design his computer programs anywhere, even in a town where he had to dodge old memories at every turn.

By the time he'd come back to Winding River, Cassie Collins had been gone, and no one was saying where. Up until then her mother had been kind to him, standing in for the mother he'd lost at an early age. But when he'd gone to see her on his return, Edna Collins had slammed the door in his face. He hadn't understood why, but he hadn't forced the issue.

Over the years he'd heard Cassie's name mentioned, usually in connection with some wild, reckless stunt that had been exaggerated by time. He'd debated questioning her best friends when they occasionally passed through town, but he'd told himself that if he'd meant anything at all to Cassie, she would have responded differently to his note. Maybe she'd just viewed that summer as a wild fling. Maybe he was the only one who'd seen it as something more. Either way, it was probably for the best to leave things as they were. Wherever she was, she was no doubt happily married by now.

When he was doing some of his rare soul-searching, Cole could admit that the romance had been ill fated from the beginning. He and Cassie were as different as two people could be. Until they'd met, he'd been the classic nerd, both studious and shy. Only an innate athletic ability and the Davis name had made him popular.

Cassie, with her warmth and exuberance and try-anything mentality, had brought out an unexpected wild streak in him. He would have done anything to earn one of her devastating smiles. The summer they had spent together had been the best time of his life. Just the memory of it was enough to stir more lust than any flesh-and-blood woman had for quite some time.

He brought himself up short. Those days were long past, and it was definitely best not to go back there.

"Well?" his father demanded. "Don't you have anything to say about that?"

"Leave it alone, Pop. The quickest way to get rid of me is to start bringing up old news."

"I hear she's coming back to town for this big reunion the school has planned," his father said, his expression sly. "Is that news current enough for you?"

Cole didn't like the way his pulse reacted to the announcement. It ricocheted as if he'd just been told that his company had outearned Microsoft.

"That has nothing to do with me," he insisted.

"She's not married."

Cole ignored that, though he was forced to concede that his heart started beating double time at the news.

"Has a son she's raising on her own," his father added.

"You know, I think you missed your calling," Cole said. "You should have started a newspaper. You seem to know all the gossip in town."

"You saying you're not interested?"

Cole met his father's gaze without flinching. "That's what I'm telling you."

Frank gave a little nod. "Okay, then. How about a game of poker tonight? I could call a few men. Have 'em out here in an hour."

Though he was relieved that his father had suddenly switched gears, Cole's gaze narrowed suspiciously. "Why would you want to do that?"

A grin spread across Frank Davis's face. "'Cause a man who can lie with a straight face the way you just did is wasting it if he's not playing a high-stakes game of cards."

Chapter Two

As she and Jake drove through the Snowy Range toward Winding River two months later, Joshua Cartwright's words played over and over in Cassie's head like the refrain from some country music tune. Going home, even temporarily, wasn't nearly as simple as he'd made it sound, which was why she'd flatly refused to pack up everything she owned and bring it with her. Once she decided whether to stay—*if* she decided to stay—she would go back for the rest of her belongings.

Meantime, with every familiar landmark she passed, her pulse escalated and her palms began to sweat. Time hadn't dulled any of her trepidation.

Jake, however, had no such qualms. He was literally bouncing on the seat in his enthusiasm, taking in everything, commenting on most of it until she wanted to scream at him to be quiet. Nerves, she told herself. It was just nerves. Jake wasn't doing anything wrong.

In fact, it was good that he was so excited. There had been far too few adventures in his young life. And it had been four years, she reminded herself. He'd been only five on their last brief visit. This all seemed as new and exciting to him as it was terrifying to her.

"How far now?" he asked for the hundredth time.

Cassie managed a thin smile. "About ten miles less than the last time you asked. We'll be there by lunchtime."

"And all these ranches, the great big ones, belong to people you know?"

"Most of them," she conceded.

She dreaded the moment when the wrought-iron gate for the Double D came into sight. Frank Davis had named it that the day his son was born, anticipating the time when the two of them would run it together. He'd never envisioned his son bringing home the daughter of a woman who took in mending. If anything, he'd wanted Cole to marry someone whose neighboring land could be added to the holdings of the Double D.

Unfortunately for him, Cole had never looked twice at their neighbors' daughters. She wondered, though, if that had changed, if Frank had gotten his way.

As the road twisted and turned, the snow-capped mountains gave way to rolling foothills. Black Angus cattle dotted the landscape. Bubbling streams and a broader, winding river cut through the land, the banks lined by thick stands of leafy cottonwoods.

Eventually the road dipped, went over a narrow span of bridge, and there it was, the town in which she'd grown up, complete with the water tower she'd once climbed and repainted shocking pink. It was a pristine white now, with flowing blue script proudly spelling out Winding River and, beneath that, in bolder letters: WELCOME.

A sign by the side of the road proudly announced the population at 1,939. If she decided to stay, would it soon be altered to say 1,941? Cassie wondered. Or would the ebb and flow of births and deaths, departures and new arrivals, keep it forever the same?

"Mom, look," Jake said in an awestruck tone.

"What?"

"Over there," he said, pointing to something she'd never seen before.

It was an airstrip, not much by big-city standards, but there were half a dozen very fancy private planes parked outside the hangar. Obviously over the past ten years some folks with money had settled in Winding River. Years ago a few of the ranchers, Cole's father among them, had kept small planes for making rapid inspections of their far-flung land, but nothing like these.

"Awesome," Jake declared, his eyes as big as saucers.

"Awesome," Cassie was forced to agree, even as she wondered at the implication.

Her mother hadn't mentioned anything to suggest that big changes were taking place in town, but then Edna Collins wasn't the kind to take stock of her surroundings or to comment on them. She stayed mostly to herself, spending her time on the mending she did to make ends meet and on church work. Because she was relieved to no longer be the target of it herself, she didn't indulge in gossip. Cassie regretted not asking more questions since her last trip home. Even her mother had to have noticed an influx of wealthy newcomers.

"Can we drive through town before we go to Grandma's?" Jake pleaded. "I've forgotten what it was like. Besides, I'm starved. Grandma won't have anything but peanut butter and jelly."

"Which she is expecting you to eat," Cassie reminded him, grateful for the excuse to put off the moment when she would have to start seeing people, facing their curious stares and blunt questions.

"We'll go into town after lunch," she promised, grinning at him. "You can have ice cream for dessert."

The promise was enough to pacify Jake, and it bought her some time…time to ask questions, time to brace herself for the possibility of running into Jake's father.

Time to get used to the increasingly likely possibility that this was going to be home again.

Cole was mending fences near the highway when the old blue sedan sped past. It said a lot about his state of mind that he even looked up. Usually his concentration was intent on the task at hand, but ever since his father's sly comment about Cassie's return, passing cars had caught his interest.

This time there was no mistaking the thick brown hair caught up in a ponytail and pulled through the opening of a baseball cap. Cassie had worn her hair exactly that way on too many occasions, making his fingers itch to free it and watch it tumble to her shoulders in silky waves. His belly tightened and his hand trembled unmistakably, either at the memory or the glimpse of her. Maybe both.

He forced his attention back to the fence, aimed his hammer at the nail with too much force and too little concentration and caught his thumb instead. His muttered expletive carried across the field to his father, who stared at him with that smug expression that had become increasingly familiar lately.

"See something interesting?" his father inquired tartly.

"Not a thing," Cole insisted, though the image of Cassie with the breeze stealing wisps of hair to tease her cheeks was firmly planted in his head. If a glimpse could tie him up in knots, what would seeing her up close do to him? He didn't want to find out.

He just needed to make himself scarce for a few days and she'd be gone again, back to wherever she lived, taking that mysterious boy of hers with her. Then his life would return to normal. His days would be uncomplicated. His nights...well, they might be boring from a social perspective, but they would be rewarding financially. He did his best work in the middle of the night when the day's stresses faded and his mind could wander.

"You going into town this afternoon?" his father asked, his expression neutral.

"Hadn't planned to."

"We could use an order of feed."

"Then pick up the phone and order it," Cole retorted, refusing to take the less-than-subtle bait.

"Just thought you might have other business to see to."

"I do," he agreed, tossing his tools into the back of the pickup. "If you need me, I'll be at the house."

His father stared at him with a disgusted expression. "Working on that blasted computer, I suppose."

"Exactly."

With any luck he could create a computer game in

which the meddling owner of a ranch was murdered by his put-upon son and nobody caught on.

From the moment she drove into the driveway at her mother's place, Cassie was taken back in time. Nothing had changed. The little white house, not much more than a cottage, really, still had a sagging porch and needed paint. As always, there was a pot of struggling red geraniums in need of water on the steps. A swing hung from a sturdy but rusting chain. The white paint had long since chipped away, leaving the swing a weathered gray.

Inside, the walls were a faded cream, the drapes too dark and heavy, as if her mother was determined to shut out the world that had never been kind to her. A sewing basket, overflowing with colorful threads, sat beside the worn chair where her mother liked to work under a bare hundred-watt bulb.

They left Jake glued to the TV and went down the hall with the luggage. Cassie discovered her room still had posters of her favorite musicians on the walls and a Denver Broncos bedspread on one twin bed. She'd bought that navy-blue and orange spread as a rebellion against the pink paint and ruffled curtains her mother had insisted on. The second bed still had a frilly, flowered spread on it. Cassie suspected its mate was still shoved in the back of the closet, where she'd put it years ago.

"I haven't changed anything," her mother said, twisting her hands nervously. "I thought you'd like to know that home was always going to be the way you remembered it."

Cassie didn't have the heart to say that some things were best forgotten. Instead she gave her mother a fierce hug. For all of her flaws this woman had done her best to give Cassie a good life. She'd lost her husband in a freak accident at a grain elevator when Cassie was little more than a toddler, but she'd found a way to be a stay-at-home mom and keep food on the table. And despite her private disapproval of her daughter's behavior and the occasional long-suffering sighs, she hadn't turned her back on Cassie, not ever.

"Thanks, Mom," she said, finally acknowledging what was long overdue.

Her mother looked startled and faintly pleased, but her face quickly assumed its more familiar neutral mask. "Will you and Jake be okay in here? You won't mind sharing a room?"

"Of course not. This will be fine. We're just glad to be here."

"Are you?" her mother asked, peering at her intently. "It's been a long time."

"Too long," Cassie agreed, studying her mother's face and seeing new wrinkles. There was more gray in her hair, too. "Jake and I have missed you."

That pleased look came and went in a heartbeat. "Will your friends be home for the reunion?" Edna asked, retreating as always to a less emotional topic.

"I haven't spoken to any of them recently. I hope so. It would be wonderful to see them again."

Her mother shook her head. "I can't imagine what Lauren must be like. Do you suppose all that fame has gone to her head? She certainly hasn't spent a dime of the money she's making on her folks. That house of theirs is tumbling down around them."

"Don't blame Lauren," Cassie said. "Her parents wouldn't take anything from her. They said an acting career was too precarious and she needed to save every last cent in case it didn't last. Lauren hired a carpenter and sent him over, but her parents just sent him away."

"That father of hers always was a stubborn old coot," Edna said. "Still, all the attention she gets from TV and the newspapers must have changed her some."

Cassie chuckled. "Lauren never cared about fame or money. I'm sure she's as surprised as the rest of us about the turn her life has taken."

"Well, Hollywood has a way of changing people. That's all I'm saying," her mother replied, disapproval written all over her face.

"Not Lauren," Cassie said with absolute confidence. If any of them had her head on straight, it was Lauren. She was always the one to express caution when a prank threatened to get out of hand, always the one who came up with a thoughtful gesture to make amends when someone's feelings were hurt.

"I suppose you know her better than I do," her mother said, though her doubts were still evident. "Are you hungry? I've made some sandwiches, and there are cookies. Mildred brought them by this morning. Oatmeal-raisin. Your favorite, if I'm not mistaken."

"Mildred's oatmeal-raisin cookies were always the best," Cassie enthused. And their neighbor had always come up with excuses for bringing over a plateful to share with a little girl whose own mother rarely baked. Those treats had earned Mildred a special place in Cassie's heart. "I'll have to stop by later to thank her."

"She'd like that. She doesn't get out much these days. Her arthritis makes it difficult for her to get around. Jake can stay with me while you and Mildred visit."

Cassie's gaze narrowed. "Don't you think Mildred would like to see your grandson?"

"There's nothing for a boy to do over there. He'd be bored," Edna responded.

She said it in a hurried way that told Cassie she was only making up hasty excuses. "Mom, I can't keep Jake hidden away in the house while we're here."

For an instant her mother looked ashamed. "No, of course not. I never meant to imply that you should."

"Surely people have gotten over what happened by now."

"Yes, I'm sure you're right. It's just that..."

Cassie met her gaze evenly. She had known they were going to have to face this. Now was as good a time as any. "What?" she asked, prepared for battle.

"He looks so much like his father now."

That was the last thing Cassie had expected her mother to say, but it was true. Jake did look like Cole, from his sun-streaked hair to his blue eyes, from those freckles across his nose to the shape of his mouth. Even the glasses were a reminder of the ones Cole had worn until high school, when he'd finally been persuaded to trade them for contacts.

Cole had been a self-described skinny, awkward geek until he'd gone away to college. There he'd begun to fill out, his body becoming less awkward and lanky. And after a summer at home working the ranch, his lean body had been all hard muscle by the time they'd started dating in earnest. Cassie imagined the same thing would happen to Jake one day, and that he would be breaking girl's hearts just like his daddy had.

The shock, of course, was that her mother could see all that. "You know," Cassie said flatly.

It was her mother's turn to look startled. "Did you think I didn't?"

"You never said a word."

Her mother shrugged. "There was nothing to say. What was done was done. No point in talking about it."

Cassie sank down on the bed, her thoughts in turmoil. All this time her mother had known the truth. She met Edna's gaze.

"Is Cole...?" Her voice trailed off.

"He's here," her mother said tightly. "Has been ever since college. He came back to help out when Frank had a heart attack. If you ask me, the man talked himself into getting sick just to manipulate that boy, but they seem to be getting on well enough out there."

Another secret kept, Cassie thought, just as she'd kept Cole's identity a secret from Jake. Why did it surprise her that her mother could be reticent about something so important? Edna had always kept her own counsel, never saying more than the situation required for politeness. Even now she didn't elaborate. If Cassie wanted to know more, she was going to have to ask directly.

"Is he married?" she asked, not sure she wanted to hear the answer.

"No."

Relief warred with surprise. Cole must be the county's prize catch. How had he managed to elude all the single women of Winding River and their ambitious parents, especially with Frank Davis no doubt pressuring him to produce an heir?

It didn't matter, she told herself sternly. It had nothing to do with her, except that it complicated her situation that Cole was still living right here. How could she possibly keep him from finding out that Jake was his son if he was practically underfoot? And if he did figure it out, what would his reaction be? Would he pretend ignorance or would he want to claim his son? She wasn't sure which thought terrified her more. Explaining to Jake that his father was here when she'd always been so elusive about his whereabouts wouldn't be any easier.

"Hey, Mom, can we eat? I'm starved."

Jake's voice cut into her thoughts. Struggling with the unexpected taste of fear in her mouth, Cassie stayed silent a minute too long, drawing a puzzled look from her son and an understanding one from her mother.

"I'll get him his sandwich," her mother offered. "You spend a few minutes unpacking and getting settled."

She followed Jake from the room, then turned back. "Give some thought to what I said. The Davises are powerful people, and Cole's got a streak of his daddy in him—no matter how you once thought otherwise. They take what's theirs."

Cassie understood the warning and all its implications. If Emma, now an attorney was coming to the reunion, Cassie would talk to her the second she arrived. Surely Emma would be able to give her some advice on how to protect her rights where Jake was concerned.

And if what her friend had to say wasn't reassuring, Cassie would take her son and leave. Perhaps she couldn't go back to work for Earlene, but they could move someplace entirely new. Cheyenne, maybe. Or Laramie. Maybe all the way north to someplace like Jackson Hole. A fresh start in a whole new town wouldn't be easy, but if it was necessary to keep her son away from Cole, Cassie would do it and never look back.

Just then the phone rang, and a moment later her

mother poked her head into the bedroom. "It's Karen. She heard you were back. Somebody in town must have seen you drive through."

A smile spread across Cassie's face as she walked down the hall to the little alcove where the old-fashioned black phone still sat on a rickety mahogany table. The first of the Calamity Janes was checking in.

"Hey, cowgirl, how are you?" she asked Karen. "And how's that handsome husband of yours?"

"Working too hard. We both are."

"But you'll be here for the reunion?"

"I wouldn't miss it."

"And the others? Have you heard from any of them?"

"They're all coming. In fact, that's why I'm calling. Lunch tomorrow at Stella's. I've told her to put a reserved sign on our favorite table in the back. Can you be there at noon?"

"I can't wait," Cassie said truthfully. "You have no idea how much I've missed you guys."

"Same here," Karen said. "And we're counting on you to think of something outrageous we can do to make this reunion as memorable as all our years in high school."

"Not me," Cassie said fervently. "I'm older and wiser now."

"And a mother," Karen said quietly. "How's Jake?"

"He's the best thing I ever did."

"And Cole? He's here, you know."

"I know."

"What will you do if you run into him?"

Cassie sighed. "I wish I knew."

"Maybe it's time to tell him the truth. I always

thought you were making a mistake in not doing that in the beginning. He loved you.''

"He used me."

"No," Karen said. "Anyone who ever saw the two of you together knew better than that. How you could miss it is beyond me.''

"He left me without a word," Cassie reminded her.

"A mistake," Karen agreed. "But you compounded it."

"How?"

"By giving up on him. By never asking what happened. By running away. For a girl who had more gumption than anyone I knew, you wimped out when it really counted.''

It was an old argument, but it still put Cassie on the defensive. "I had no choice," she insisted.

"Oh, sweetie, we all have choices," she said, sounding suddenly tired.

The hint of exhaustion was so unlike the ex-cheerleader that it startled Cassie. If she'd been a ringleader, Karen had always been her most energetic sidekick, always eager for a lark.

"Karen, are you okay? Is everything all right at the ranch?"

"Just too much work and too little time."

"But you and Caleb are happy, right?"

"Blissfully, at least when we can stay awake long enough to remember why we got married in the first place." She sighed. "Don't listen to me. I love my life. I wouldn't trade it for anything. And I will tell you every last, boring detail when I see you tomorrow.''

"Love you, pal."

"You, too. I can't wait to see you. Bring Jake along. I want to see if he's as handsome as his daddy."

"Not tomorrow. Can you imagine a nine-year-old listening to us talk about old times? Besides, it might give him ideas."

"Meaning?"

"Meaning he gets into enough mischief without getting any tips from us. And I'll tell you *that* story when I see you."

As she hung up the phone, she suddenly felt as if all her fears and cares had slipped away. The Calamity Janes were getting together tomorrow. Let Cole find out about Jake and do his worst. She had backup on the way. And together, the Calamity Janes were indomitable.

Chapter Three

The door to Cole's home office burst open, and his father charged in as if he were on a mission. Normally Cole would have protested the intrusion into his private sanctuary, but he was too exhausted. He'd been up all night putting the finishing touches on a program that would revolutionize the way businesses interconnected on the Internet. His gut told him it was going to be the most lucrative bit of technology he'd ever created.

"What?" he asked as his father loomed over him, a frown on his face as he studied the computer screen.

"Is that supposed to make sense?" Frank asked, leaning down for a closer look.

"Not to you, but to another computer it's magic," Cole said.

"Guess I'll have to take your word on that."

"I'm sure you didn't barge in here to talk about computers," Cole said dryly. "What's on your mind?

You're usually in town at Stella's at this hour swapping lies with all your buddies.''

"Been there. Now I'm back.''

"I see,'' Cole said. "And you're what? Reporting in with the latest Winding River gossip?''

"Don't sass me, son. I did happen to pick up a little bit of news I thought might interest you.''

"Unless it's a way to squeeze eight hours of sleep into the two hours I have before I meet with Don Rollins about that bull you want, I doubt it.''

Undaunted, his father announced, "Cassie and her friends will be at Stella's at noon today. Stella's about to bust a gusset at the thought that a famous movie star is going to be dining in her establishment. That's what she said, 'dining in my establishment.' Talk about putting on airs. She's talking about little Lauren Winters. We've known the girl since she was in diapers. I can't see what all the ruckus is about.''

He shook his head. "Well, never mind about that. The point is that Cassie will be there.''

Cole's pulse did a little hop, skip and jump, which he resolutely blamed on exhaustion. "So?''

"Just thought you'd want to know.''

"And now I do.'' He stared evenly at his father. "Are you waiting for some sort of reaction?''

"As a matter of fact, I am. Any hot-blooded son of mine would take a shower, shave, splash on a little of that fancy aftershave women like and haul his butt into town. Now's your chance, son. Don't waste it.''

"I'm confused about something. When did you become such a big fan of Cassie's?''

Guilt flickered in his father's eyes for an instant before he shrugged. "The point is *you* cared about her once.''

"A long time ago. You saw to it that it came to nothing."

"Well, maybe I regret that."

"Do you really?" Cole asked doubtfully, then shook his head. "Look, forget it. I have an appointment, anyway."

"I can buy my own blasted bull," his father retorted. "Seems to me like you ought to have better fish to fry."

Cole raked a hand through his hair, spared one last glance at the computer screen before shutting it down, then stood up.

"A shower sounds good," he conceded. "As for the rest, if I were you, I'd be real careful about telling me how capable you are of managing without me. I might get the idea that I could leave this ranch and Winding River and you wouldn't even miss me."

His father began to sputter a lot of nonsense about not saying any such thing, but Cole ignored the protest and headed upstairs for a long, hot shower to work out the kinks in his neck and shoulders. Given the state of his thoughts about Cassie Collins, he probably should have let the water run cold.

An hour later, feeling moderately more alive, he left the house and headed into town. Not to satisfy his father, he assured himself. Not even to catch a glimpse of Cassie. Just to grab a decent meal that he didn't have to cook himself, maybe pick up a few things at the feed and grain store. If Cassie happened to be around, well, that was pure coincidence, the kind of thing that happened in small towns. People bumped into people all the time, exchanged a few words, then went on about their business. It didn't have to mean a thing.

Yeah, right. He sneezed as he caught a whiff of that

aftershave he'd splashed on at the last minute. He yanked a handkerchief out of his pocket and rubbed at his cheeks, but the scent stayed with him, mocking his avowed intentions about this trip into town.

He glanced in the rearview mirror of his truck, assured himself that no one was behind him, then slammed on the brakes right there in the middle of the highway. He could quit lying to himself right now, turn around, go back to the ranch and take that nap he'd been craving before his father had shown up. And if he wanted to salvage a lick of pride, that was exactly what he ought to do.

"Do it," he muttered. "Be sensible for once in your miserable life."

But the lure of seeing Cassie again was too much to ignore. It had been a long time since he'd let temptation get the better of him. Surely he could be forgiven a single lapse.

With a sigh he took his foot off the brake and kept going, heading straight for trouble.

"Oh, my word, I never thought I'd see all of you back together again," Stella Partlow said, hands on her ample hips as her gaze circled the table at the back of her diner. "These class reunions always take me right back. Not a one of you has changed a lick."

"Not even Lauren?" Cassie asked the woman who had given her her first job as a waitress back in high school. Stella had ignored the gossip and patiently gone about the business of turning Cassie into a responsible employee.

At Cassie's question, Stella peered intently at Lauren, then shook her head. "Nope. She was always a beauty. Back then she just didn't make the most of the looks God gave her. I've always said a good haircut and a few beauty products can turn the plainest woman into something a man can't resist."

"You still selling Avon?" Emma teased.

"Well, of course I am," Stella retorted. "But right this second I'm pushing hamburgers. How about five with the works, just the way you used to like 'em?"

"And fries," Karen said with a gleam of anticipation in her eyes.

"And chocolate milk shakes," Cassie added, all but licking her lips. Nobody anywhere made shakes as thick and rich as Stella's. Not even Earlene had the knack.

"Except for me," Lauren corrected.

"I imagine you'll be having a cherry cola, same as always," Stella said, giving her a wink. "Coming right up. You all try to keep the noise level down back here. I've got tourists, and they like a little peace and quiet while they eat."

"I'll bet if you point out that they're in the presence of a gen-u-ine movie star, they won't care how much racket we make," Gina told her.

Lauren frowned. "Stop it, you guys. Acting's a job. It's not who I am. If anybody ought to know that, you should," she reminded them.

Cassie thought she detected an edge in her friend's voice, but Lauren laughed just as hard as the rest of them at the teasing comments that followed. And when they plagued her with questions about her leading men, her responses were as ribald as the discussions they'd had about boys in high school.

When their drinks came, Cassie raised her glass. "A toast. To the Calamity Janes—may all our troubles be behind us."

Just as the others joined in, Cassie's glance strayed to the window looking onto Main Street. Cole Davis was standing on the sidewalk staring right back at her, his hands jammed in the pockets of his faded denims, his jaw set and an unreadable expression in his eyes.

"Uh-oh," Karen murmured. "Looks as if that toast came too late. Trouble is about to come calling."

All of the women followed Cole's progress as he strode to the door and entered the diner.

Cassie swallowed hard and prayed that she wouldn't make a complete fool of herself. It was just a chance meeting with an old flame. Nothing more. Nothing to cause this churning in the pit of her stomach. There was no reason for her heart to slam against her ribs or her pulse to ricochet wildly. Jake was safely at home with her mother, so there was no reason for this little lick of fear that was sliding up the back of her throat.

Get a grip, she told herself mentally as she lifted her gaze to meet his. Those unflinching blue eyes were just as devastating as ever. Her stomach flipped over. Her heart pounded. Her pulse ricocheted. Reason apparently had nothing to do with anything where Cole was concerned, not even after ten long years.

Tension swirled as she felt four gazes pinned on her, waiting to see what she would do. She drew in a deep breath and reminded herself she was a grown-up woman—a mother, in fact. She could handle a simple little exchange with a man, even if he did happen to be the father of the child she'd kept from him...even if she'd spent years nurturing her hatred of him.

"Cole," she acknowledged with a slight nod.

"Cassie."

His voice was as low and sexy as she'd remembered, his face more mature, his lips in that same straight line that had always dared her to try to coax a smile from him. His blue eyes were as cold as a wintry sky, though why they were eluded her. *He* was the one who'd walked out on *her.* If anyone had a right to be fuming mad, it was she. He ought to be on his knees apologizing, which was about as likely as the sun starting to rise in the west.

When it looked as if the conversation had run into a dead end before getting off the ground, Karen, ever the peacemaker, jumped in.

"How's Frank?" she asked, as if the tension weren't already thick enough without bringing up Cole's father.

"Same as ever. Cantankerous," he said, bestowing the smile on her that he'd refused Cassie.

"Still grumbling about getting you married off?" Karen teased. Cassie poked an elbow sharply in her ribs.

"The topic does come up now and again," Cole said, amusement tilting the corners of his mouth.

"Your father always gets his way in the end," Gina chimed in. "I don't see why you don't just get it over with. The way I hear it from my folks, every female in ten counties is after you."

Cole grinned at her, a full-fledged smile, capable of breaking hearts. "Including you? How about it, Gina? Are you available?"

Cassie scowled as she waited for her friend's reply.

"If you'd asked a week ago, I'd have turned you down flat," Gina said. "Now, who knows?"

The flip remark drew stares from the others. Something wasn't right with Gina, either. Cassie had sensed it from the moment they'd sat down, but there hadn't been time to get into it. Whatever it was, it had to be serious for her to even joke about a willingness to leave her beloved New York and stay in Wyoming.

Cassie couldn't give the matter any more thought just then, though, because she glanced up and spotted Jake and his grandmother coming across the street. After their talk yesterday, Cassie had thought there was no way her mother would bring the boy into town, but she'd clearly underestimated Jake's powers of persuasion. He'd been pestering them for ice cream ever since Cassie had reneged on her promise of it the day before.

A sense of dread filled her as she watched their progress. She did not want Cole meeting her son—not today, not ever—though that was likely to be tricky if she decided she was back home to stay. After the awkwardness of the past few minutes, she was beginning to see that staying in Winding River might not be feasible. She couldn't live with the kind of panic that had streaked through her when she'd seen Jake unwittingly heading straight toward his daddy.

"You guys, I have to run," she said, dropping some money on the table and slipping out of the booth. "I have to get home."

"But our food..." Lauren began, then glanced outside and fell silent.

Cassie circled around behind Cole, giving him a wide berth, hoping that her friends would keep him occupied just long enough for her to catch Jake and her mother and detour them away from the restaurant.

"I'll call you," Karen said.

"And we'll see you tomorrow night," Lauren added.

"Absolutely. I can't wait," she said before dashing off to intercept her son.

She was dismayed when she realized Cole had fallen

into step beside her. Just outside the door, he gazed down into her eyes, his expression vaguely troubled.

"Why the sudden rush, Cassie? I didn't scare you off, did I?"

His tone mocked her, but there was that contradictory flicker of concern in his eyes. She didn't know what to make of either, and right now she didn't have time to grapple with it. Disaster was less than half a block away.

"Of course not," she said a little too sharply. "I just have to get home, that's all. I promised my mother I wouldn't be gone long."

His expression softened. "How's your mother doing?" he asked with apparent sincerity.

Cassie thought back to the special bond Cole and her mom had shared. It, too, had died when Cole abandoned Cassie. If she were a more generous person, Cassie mused, she might regret that. Cole, who'd lost his own mother at an early age, had basked in the attention Edna had given him.

Cassie glanced outside and saw that her mother was disappearing through a door down the street. Apparently she'd caught a glimpse of Cole and wisely hurried Jake toward the trendy new restaurant and coffee bar Cassie had noticed earlier. Cassie breathed a sigh of relief and turned her gaze back to Cole.

"Fine," she said. "My mother's just fine."

He seemed startled by that. "Really?"

Something in his voice told Cassie he knew something she didn't. She stared at him intently. "Why did you say that like that?"

He evaded her gaze, his expression suddenly uneasy. "Like what?"

"Stop it, Cole. Don't play games with me. Is there

something going on with my mother that I don't know about? Is she keeping something from me?''

''You'll have to ask her that.''

All thoughts of Cole's near-miss encounter with his son fled as she stared at him and tried to read his deliberately enigmatic expression. He was hiding something. It was plain as day. ''Dammit, Cole. Tell me.''

''I just inquired after your mother, Cassie. I was being polite,'' he insisted mildly. ''Don't read anything more into it.''

''Nothing with you is ever that simple.''

''You're a fine one to talk.''

Her temper flared, and her gaze clashed with his. ''What is *that* supposed to mean?''

''Nothing. Never mind. There's no point in dredging up old news.'' He bit back a curse, then shook his head. ''I knew coming into town today was a mistake.''

Cassie was startled by the note of betrayal in his voice. ''Have you been rewriting history, Cole? *You* left *me*. It wasn't the other way around.''

''Wasn't it?'' he asked with unmistakable resentment.

Her own bitter memories, always just beneath the surface, bubbled up. ''How can you ask that? One night you were making love to me, telling me how incredible I was, the next day you were gone.''

''I explained that.''

''Explained it?'' she repeated incredulously. ''When was that? Until you walked through the door at Stella's a few minutes ago, I hadn't seen or heard from you since the night you stole my virginity.''

He winced. ''Dammit, Cassie, it wasn't like that. I didn't steal anything. We made love. It was a mutual decision. Besides, I left you a note. I know you got it, because you sent me an answer. Do I have to remind you what was in it? You said you wanted nothing more to do with me, that I should go back to college and forget all about you. You said you intended to get on with your life and that I was no longer a part of it.''

Disbelief washed over her. This was ridiculous. Why would he make up such an absurd lie? No doubt to soothe his own conscience.

''I never wrote such a note and you know it.''

''Really?'' he said scathingly. ''Remind me to show it to you sometime. I've kept it all these years as a reminder not to trust a woman's pretty words of love, especially when she says them in my bed.''

Before she could recover, he turned on his heel and walked away, leaving Cassie staring after him, wide-eyed with shock. Not one single word he'd said made a lick of sense. She'd never gotten any letter from him. Nor had she sent a reply. But it was clear that Cole believed otherwise.

She felt a blast of cool air as the door to Stella's opened behind her. ''You okay?'' Gina asked, draping an arm around her shoulders.

''I'm...'' She thought about what had just happened. ''Confused, I guess.''

''About what? Your feelings for Cole?''

''No. He said some things. Things that didn't make any sense.''

Gina's gaze narrowed. ''What things? If he upset you, I'll get the others and we'll beat him up for you.''

The comment drew a weak smile. They would do it, too. ''I don't think that will be necessary,'' Cassie said. ''But I love you for offering.''

''Come back inside and eat your burger.''

''I can't. I need to find Jake and my mother. I want

to make sure that Cole didn't catch a glimpse of them.''
She thought then of his odd reaction to her claim that
her mother was fine. ''I need to talk to Mom about
something else, too.''

''But you'll be at the party tomorrow, right?''

''I'll be there,'' Cassie promised. She met Gina's
gaze evenly. ''You and I need to have a long talk.''

''About?''

''Whatever's going on with you.''

''Don't worry about me,'' Gina said, giving her a
hug.

''Then what was that remark to Cole all about? You
sounded as if you might actually consider hanging
around Winding River instead of going back to New
York. I can't believe you would ever walk away from
your restaurant.''

''I was joking,'' Gina insisted. ''Surely you didn't
think I would seriously consider marrying your guy?''

''Cole's not my guy, and that wasn't the point. You
might have been joking about that, but you sounded
serious about the rest, about staying here.''

''So?'' Gina said, her expression defiant. ''It's home.
Are you telling me that the thought of staying here
hasn't crossed *your* mind since you've been back?''

''That's different.''

''How?''

''It just is,'' Cassie said. She looked up and saw Jake
and her mother emerge from the restaurant down the
block carrying ice cream cones. They caught sight of
her and headed in her direction.

''We'll finish this conversation tomorrow,'' she
warned Gina. ''I'm not buying a word you've said so
far.''

''And I'm not buying for a second that you're over

Cole Davis,'' Gina retorted. She waved at Cassie's mother, then retreated inside Stella's.

Cassie sighed. Gina was right. If she'd learned nothing else in the past half hour, it was that she was a long, long way from being over Cole Davis.

Chapter Four

"Mom!"

Grappling with the discovery that her feelings for Cole were as powerful as ever, Cassie barely registered Jake's cry. Then she felt an impatient tug on her arm and gazed down into her son's eyes, eyes the same shade of blue as those of the man who'd just dropped a bombshell, then strolled away.

"What, Jake?" she asked, still distracted by her realization that not even years of bitterness had dimmed what she'd once felt for Cole Davis. Add to that Cole's charge that she'd been at fault, that he hadn't abandoned her at all, but rather *she* had turned her back on *him*, and it was little wonder that she was confused. How could he have gotten it so wrong?

"Mom!" Jake said impatiently. "You're not listening."

"I'm sorry," she said, turning her attention to him.

"Do you know who that was?" Jake demanded, his cheeks flushed with excitement, his eyes sparkling.

Her heart seemed to slam to a stop. "Who?" she asked cautiously, fighting panic.

Had Jake guessed? Had he seen the resemblance between himself and the man with whom she'd been talking? Would a nine-year-old be intuitive enough to guess that a stranger was his father?

A quick glance at her mother reassured her. Her mother gave a slight shake of her head, indicating that so far her secret was safe, both from Cole and her son. No, this was about something else, though she couldn't imagine what.

"That man you were talking to," Jake explained. "Do you know who he is?"

"Of course I know. He's a rancher. He's lived here all his life."

"And you know him?" Jake demanded, clearly awestruck.

"Yes," she said slowly. Clearly she was missing something. "How do *you* know him?"

"He's Cole Davis," Jake said. "*The* Cole Davis."

When she failed to react, her son regarded her with exasperation. "Mom, you know, the guy who makes all the neat computer programs, remember? Like I told you I wanted to do someday. He's, like, the smartest guy in the whole tech world. I've told you about him, remember?"

She had a vague recollection of that, but it couldn't possibly be the same man. This Cole, *her* Cole, was a rancher, not a computer programmer. Or was he? She had no idea what he'd studied in college. Back then they'd been far too caught up in their hormones to spend a lot of time talking about Cole's plans for the future.

"Are you sure, honey? Cole's from a ranching family. His father owns the biggest spread in this county."

"I know. I read all about it on the Internet. It is so awesome that you actually know him." He turned to his grandmother. "Do you know him, too?"

She nodded, looking distraught.

"Will you introduce me?" Jake begged Cassie.

"No," she said so sharply that Jake's eyes filled with tears.

"Why not?" he asked, practically quivering with indignation.

Because she couldn't risk it. If Cole was furious with her because of a letter she'd known nothing about, how would he react to the news that she'd kept his son from him? And then there was Frank Davis. How would he react to the news that a Davis heir had been kept from *him?*

"Because we're not going to be here long enough," she said, making up her mind that staying in Winding River was impossible. "Besides, if what you say is true, I'm sure he's a very busy man. I doubt we'll even bump into him again."

The crestfallen look on Jake's face cut straight through her. He asked for so little, and she was denying him something that was evidently very important to him.

"I'm sorry, Jake."

"You're not sorry," he shouted, letting his ice cream cone tumble to the ground. "You're not sorry at all."

He took off at a run, blindly heading in the very same direction in which his father had gone only moments before. Dear God, what if Cole hadn't left? What if he were in a store and chose that precise moment to exit? Jake would take matters into his own hands. He would force an introduction.

Cassie raced after Jake, commanding him to stop.

He was at the end of Main Street before his pace faltered. She caught up with him there. Breathless, she tilted his chin up to gaze at his tear-streaked face.

"I'm sorry, baby. I truly am." She wrapped her arms around her son and let him sob out his unhappiness, regretting that she couldn't grant his seemingly simple request. How much worse would his anger at her be if he ever discovered the truth—that she was not only keeping him from a hero, but from his own father?

"I don't get it," Jake whispered. "If you know him, why can't I just meet him? It's not like I'd pester him with a million questions."

Cassie actually found herself grinning at that as she brushed the hair back from his forehead. "Oh, no? You *always* have a million questions."

"But I wouldn't ask them. I swear it."

"Sweetie, if I could make it happen, I would."

His expression turned mulish again. "You could. You just don't want to. And you said we were gonna stay at Grandma's a long time, so there's plenty of time."

Apparently, he hadn't picked up on her earlier comment about leaving...or else he'd chosen to ignore it because it hadn't suited him.

"I've been thinking about that," she admitted slowly. "I think we should leave right after the reunion." She forced a smile. "How about going to Cheyenne? Wouldn't you like to live in a big city for a change, Jake? Just think about it. It's the capital of the state, and in the summer there are Frontier Days. You've asked about that.''

Jake pushed away from her, that look of betrayal back in his eyes. ''No. I don't want to live in Cheyenne. I want to stay here. You promised. When you said goodbye to Earlene, you said you weren't ever coming back except to pick up our things. That meant we were gonna stay here.''

''I didn't promise. I said it was something we might consider. I've thought it over, and I think it's a bad idea.''

''Don't I get a say?''

''Not about this.''

''Well, I won't go. You do whatever you want. Grandma will let me stay with her.''

Cassie knew better, but she let it pass. Once Jake calmed down, she would make him see how exciting it would be to move to Cheyenne, even though she dreaded the prospect herself.

''Come on. Let's go find Grandma,'' she said, taking his hand. He yanked it away, but he did come with her.

She could see her mother still waiting in front of Stella's, leaning against the bumper of a pickup, her face pale except for too-bright patches of color in her cheeks. There was a sheen of perspiration on Edna's brow. Cole's offhand remarks flooded back to Cassie. She studied her mother.

''Mom, are you okay?''

''I'm fine. It's just a little hotter out here than I thought.''

Was it that or something more? Was her imagination running wild? After all, it *was* hot. She was perspiring herself. ''Let's go inside and get you something cold to drink,'' Cassie suggested.

"No, I'd rather go home. If you'll get the car..." Edna's voice trailed off.

Cassie regarded her worriedly. The request was a totally uncharacteristic sign of weakness. "Of course I will. Where did you park?"

"I can show you," Jake said.

"No, you stay right here with your grandmother in case she needs anything. I'll find the car."

"It's just around the corner," her mother said, handing her the keys.

Cassie ran all the way to the car. She hadn't liked the way her mother looked. Worse, Edna Collins never admitted to an illness of any kind. She had borne everything from colds to appendicitis with stoic resolve during Cassie's childhood. For her to ask Cassie to get the car, rather than coming along with her, was an incredible admission.

Cassie found the car parked in front of Dolly's Hair Salon, whipped it out of the tight parking space and was back at Stella's in less than five minutes. Her mother all but collapsed into the front seat.

"That air-conditioning sure feels good," she said to Cassie. Then, as if determined to reassure her daughter, she added, "The heat just got to me for a minute. I promise that's all it was."

Cassie let the remark pass. She had no intention of discussing her mother's health with Jake sitting in the back seat, tuned in to every word. The minute they were alone, though, she was determined to get some straight answers. And if she didn't like them, she was going to call their longtime family physician and get the truth from him.

Unfortunately, her mother seemed to anticipate her

intentions and scooted straight to her room, where she all but slammed the door in Cassie's face.

"What on earth?" Cassie murmured, staring at the door.

She picked up the phone and called the doctor, only to be told he was away until the following week. Frustrated, she had barely hung up when the phone rang. She answered distractedly, then froze at the sound of Cole's voice.

"Cassie?" he repeated when she remained silent.

"What?" she said finally.

"We need to talk."

"I don't think so."

"Well, I do. I'm coming over."

She glanced at Jake, who was back in front of the TV. "No, absolutely not," she said fiercely. "I don't want you here."

"Why not, Cassie? What are you hiding?"

"I'm not hiding anything. It's my mother. She's not feeling well," she said, grasping at straws. "The last thing she needs is to have the two of us fussing right under her nose."

"Then meet me. You pick the place."

"Didn't you hear a word I said? My mother's not feeling well."

"Of course. You need to stay there for now."

He had given up too easily. That only made Cassie more suspicious.

"I'll see you at the party tomorrow night, then," he said. "We'll find some time to talk there."

"You're coming to the party?" she asked, not even trying to hide her dismay. "You weren't in our class."

He chuckled at that. "It's a small town. The reunion's a big deal. Everyone will be there, if only to get a glimpse of our big movie star.''

''But…'' Why had she never considered that possibility? What had ever made her think she could go to a reunion in Winding River and not bump into Cole everywhere she turned?

''My being there won't bother you, will it? Ten years is a long time. Whatever was between us is surely dead and buried, right?''

She heard the unmistakable taunt in his voice. ''Absolutely,'' she responded. ''It is definitely dead and buried. Just one question, though.''

''What's that?''

''If it's dead and buried, then what could you and I possibly have to talk about?''

''Just putting one last nail in the coffin to make sure it stays that way,'' he said dryly. ''I'll see you tomorrow.''

Now there was something to look forward to, she thought dully as she hung up the phone. The prospect should have terrified her, and on one level it did. His taunts should have filled her with outrage, and to a degree they did.

So why was her pulse scampering wildly out of control? Why was she suddenly wondering if there was one sexy outfit packed in her luggage? Why did she feel as if not one of the outrageous, dangerous things she'd done in high school could hold a candle to what might happen tomorrow night back in that same high school gym?

Something told her she didn't dare spend a whole lot of time considering the answers to those questions. If she did, and if she was smart, she might pack up everything and head for Cheyenne tonight.

* * *

Cole couldn't imagine what had possessed him to call Cassie, much less announce his intention of going to the reunion party. It was the last place he wanted to be. In fact, he'd ignored the invitation, though he doubted anyone would turn him away at the door as long as he showed up with the price of admission.

He blamed his last-minute change of heart on that encounter with Cassie in the street. It wasn't just the fact that her skin still looked as soft as silk. Nor did it have anything to do with the way her body had added a few lush curves over the years. And it wasn't because her hair was shot through with fire when the sunlight caught it. No, it was none of that.

It was that damnable lie she'd told him with a perfectly straight face. If he hadn't known the truth, he would have believed her—she'd been that convincing. Which meant, he concluded, that she'd believed every word she'd spoken.

Somewhere along the way something had gotten all twisted around, and he wanted to know how. Once he knew that, he could put the past to rest, put that last nail in the coffin of their love affair, just as he'd told her. Maybe she didn't care about what had happened back then, but he did. God help him.

In fact, he was so anxious to get the difficult conversation over with that he got to the gym the next night before seven, while the reunion committee was still setting up its tables outside the doors. Mimi Frances Lawson took one look at him and latched on to his arm with a death grip.

"I need you inside, Cole," she announced, dragging him along behind her. "The streamers are falling down around us, and I don't have time to deal with it. The ladder's over there." She pointed it out. "Here's a roll of tape. I don't know what Hallie used when she put them up, but it's not holding."

She leveled a look straight into his eyes, the somber look of a general sending troops into battle. "I'm counting on you to fix it."

"Yes, ma'am," he said, amused and somewhat relieved to have a task that was actually within his capabilities and not fraught with the emotional repercussions of his anticipated confrontation with Cassie.

"I mean it," Mimi Frances said with an authority that came from being class president for three years running, or maybe from being the mother of five rambunctious boys. "I'm counting on you, Cole."

"These streamers won't budge before next Christmas, Mimi Frances," he assured her. "Now go on with whatever you need to be doing and leave this to me."

She nodded. "I'll send someone in to help as soon as I can spare them."

The fact that she thought he needed help rankled a bit, but Cole ignored it and went to work. He was at the top of a ladder, balanced precariously, when he realized he was no longer alone. He looked straight down into Cassie's familiar green eyes. She stared back unhappily.

"So, Mimi Frances recruited you, too," he said mildly, all too aware that she wasn't one bit happy about being stuck with him, even in this very public setting.

"That woman could run the entire U.S. government without breaking a sweat," Cassie muttered. "I'm fairly certain I told her I was not climbing any ladders."

"Then it's fortunate she paired you up with me. I'm

not scared of heights," Cole said, trying not to stare too hard at the sexy little black dress that revealed way too much cleavage, at least from this angle.

"I'm not scared of heights, either," Cassie retorted, indignant patches of color promptly flaring in her cheeks. "I beat you to the top of the town water tower, if I remember correctly."

"So you did," he agreed, grinning. "Then what's the problem?"

"I'd like to see you climb anything in this dress."

"Honey, if I were in that dress, we'd have bigger problems at this reunion than the falling streamers."

A chuckle erupted, just as he'd intended, but she was quick to choke it back. Clearly, she wasn't quite ready for a thaw in the icy distance between them.

He gazed down at her. "Don't stop. I always liked hearing you laugh."

Her gaze narrowed. "Don't go there, Cole."

"Go where?"

"You know."

"To the past? Isn't that what this reunion is all about? Can you think of a better time to think about what used to be?"

"I suspect you and I have very different memories about what used to be."

He nodded. "Based on our conversation yesterday, I'd say you're right about that."

He was about to use the opening to pursue the topic, when Mimi Frances bustled up.

"Stop chatting," she ordered briskly. "We only have a few more minutes."

"Everything is going to go beautifully," Cassie reassured her. "The gym looks sensational. And Cole only has one or two more streamers to secure. Go outside, Mimi Frances, and take a deep breath, then sit back and enjoy yourself. You've outdone yourself. It looks prettier in here than it did on prom night—and that's saying a lot.''

''I don't have time to enjoy myself,'' Mimi Frances snapped, refusing to bask in the praise or take the advice. ''Somebody has to see to all the details. I'd like to know who it's going to be, if not me.''

''Delegate,'' Cole advised. ''You got me on this ladder, didn't you?''

Mimi Frances looked flustered for a second, then a smile spread across her face. ''Yes, I did, didn't I? Well, let me just go outside and see who's lurking about with nothing to do. Thanks, Cole.''

He gave her a wink. ''Any time, Madam President.''

Mimi Frances went off in search of more recruits. Cole came down the ladder, slid it a few feet across the floor, then turned to Cassie. ''Okay, your turn.''

''My turn?'' she echoed blankly. ''To do what?''

''You were assigned streamer duty, too. So far, I'm the only one who's done a lick of work. How could you stand there and look Mimi Frances in the eye, knowing that you hadn't done a blessed thing she asked you to? That woman is counting on us. The success of this entire reunion rests on our shoulders.''

''Oh, please,'' Cassie said with a groan. ''Besides, you're doing a fine job. I'll hold the ladder.''

''Not that I don't trust you, darlin', but I think I like the idea of *me* holding it for *you* a whole lot better.'' He handed her the tape, plucked her off the ground and set her on the first rung. ''Climb.'' He paused, his gazed locked with hers. ''Unless you really are scared of heights.''

She frowned at him, then dutifully kicked off her

shoes. She was halfway up, seemingly oblivious to the fact that her dress had hiked a good three inches up her thighs, when she paused and scowled down at him. "If I catch you looking up my skirt, Cole Davis, you're a dead man."

"The thought never crossed my mind," he lied cheerfully, then dutifully averted his gaze, at least until her back was turned.

"You can't have changed that much," she retorted, shooting daggers at him when she caught the direction of his gaze.

"Maybe I have," he said. "You haven't spent enough time with me to find out."

"And I'm not likely to," she told him, slapping a wad of tape on the streamer, then sticking it to the wall before descending.

Cole stood right at the bottom waiting for her, just far enough back to give her a little room to maneuver her way toward the floor. Then he braced one arm on either side of the ladder so that when she reached the last step she was all but in his arms.

"Want to place a bet on that?" he taunted, his mouth next to her ear. She almost tumbled off the bottom rung and into his waiting arms, just as he'd anticipated. He was starting to enjoy keeping her off balance, literally and figuratively.

"Back off," she commanded.

Cole recognized the heat in her tone. Cassie had always had a temper. It was slow to flare out of control, but once it did, it was as lively as the fireworks the town had planned for the Fourth of July. He'd missed that kind of excitement in his life.

He stood his ground. "Not just yet."

She looked over her shoulder and straight into his eyes. ''Why are you doing this?''

For the longest time he just lost himself in the depths of her furious, flashing eyes. He ignored the whisper of dismay in her voice, the cry of old wounds in his soul. Finally he sighed.

''I wish to hell I knew,'' he said softly.

Then and only then did he take a step back and, after one last lingering look, turn and walk away.

It was a strategic retreat, nothing more, he told himself. He needed to spend a little time getting his head together before he had that confrontation with her he'd been thinking about for the past two days.

Otherwise he was liable to spend the time kissing her senseless, instead of getting the answers he wanted.

Chapter Five

Cassie hadn't felt this jittery since her first date with
Cole more than ten years earlier. After he'd walked
away, when she finally managed that last shaky step
from the ladder, her knees all but buckled. She grabbed
her shoes and fled to the ladies' room. She was splash-
ing cold water on her overheated cheeks when Karen
wandered in.

"Here you are. Cole said you were around. How
long have you been here?"

"Too long," Cassie muttered.

"What?"

"Oh, never mind. I never should have come back to
Winding River."

Karen's gaze narrowed. "Is Cole giving you a rough
time? He hasn't seen Jake, has he?"

"Not yet, but wouldn't you know my son spotted
him yesterday and knew exactly who he was. Appar-

ently Cole is some hotshot computer guy, total hero material to a tech-savvy nine-year-old. Jake is furious because I won't introduce them.''

"Oh, my," Karen said, regarding her with sympathy. "That *is* a problem. Will Jake let it drop?"

"Not a chance, which is why I'm getting out of town first thing next week."

"But your mom," Karen began, then fell silent.

Cassie seized on the inadvertent slip. "What about my mother?"

"Nothing." Karen turned away to concentrate on touching up her lipstick.

Cassie regarded her with impatience. "Dammit, not you, too. Cole started this same tight-lipped routine with me yesterday. What is going on? The doctor's out of town, so I haven't been able to get any answers from him."

Karen sighed, then stepped away from the mirror to give her a fierce hug. "Talk to her."

Cassie's heart began to thud dully. There was only one thing that would have Cole and one of her dearest friends tiptoeing around. She held on to Karen and looked straight into her eyes.

"She's sick, isn't she?"

"Just talk to her," her friend repeated, then fell silent. A moment later, before Cassie could even attempt to persuade her to open up, Karen subtly sniffed the air.

"School's been out for a month. How is it possible that it still smells like sweaty gym socks in here?"

Cassie chuckled despite herself, then gestured to the array of air fresheners around the room. "Don't tell Mimi Frances. She'll die of embarrassment. Evidently she thought she'd solved that particular problem."

Karen wrinkled her nose. "Not by a long shot." She grabbed Cassie's hand. "Come on. Let's get out of here before the others come crowding in to see what's wrong. I don't know about you, but I do not intend to spend an entire evening in a room that stinks, not when there's fresh air in the gym and a great band playing all our old favorites. I get my husband to myself too seldom as it is. I intend to make the most of it."

Back in the gym, they found most of the Calamity Janes already dancing. Caleb gave Cassie a quick kiss on the cheek, then snagged his wife's hand.

"Come on, angel, let's see if you've still got those moves I remember," he said.

Cassie watched enviously as he spun Karen onto the dance floor. At least one of her friends had settled into a happy relationship, she thought. Caleb might be older than his wife, but it was evident that their match was heaven made. Once Karen had set eyes on the rancher, all her dreams of traveling the globe had taken a back seat to her desire to become his wife.

Feeling blue and alone, Cassie wandered over to the bar and ordered a soda. Something told her she was going to need a clear head tonight, if not to deal with Cole, then certainly for that dreaded conversation with her mother.

The fast song ended, and a slow, oldies ballad began. Memories of another night, hot and sultry and filled with promise, stole over her. She felt a hand on her waist, felt the whisper of warm breath against her cheek and knew it was Cole behind her.

"Does it take you back?" he asked.

To a place she didn't want to go, she thought but didn't say. "Nostalgia's a funny thing," she said instead. "It tends to take away all the rough edges and leave you with pretty images."

"Anything wrong with that?" he asked.

"It's not real. It's not the way it was. Not all of it, anyway."

He stepped in front of her, his gaze steady. "Dance with me, Cassie."

"Cole…" The protest formed in her head, but she couldn't seem to get the words out.

"For old-time's sake."

Drawn to him, caught up in the very nostalgia she'd decried, she slipped into his arms and rested her head against his chest. The feel of him, the clean, male scent, the weight of his arms circling her waist—all of it was incredibly, dangerously familiar. Their bodies fit together perfectly, moving as one to the music, connected in a way that hinted of another, far more intimate and never-forgotten unity.

"God, I've missed you," he said, his voice ragged and tinged with regret.

Was it regret for time lost, though, or for emotions he couldn't control? Cassie wondered.

The music played on for what seemed like an eternity, but when it ended at last, she thought it hadn't gone on nearly long enough. Cole released her, then captured her hand in his.

"Come on. I'll buy you a drink." He regarded her questioningly as they approached the bar. "Another soda?"

She nodded. When he had her cola and his beer, he led her outside. She didn't resist. She couldn't. It seemed they were both caught up in some sort of spell. Reunions had a way of doing that, she supposed. They were intended to take you back in time, to a simpler era when nothing mattered but football victories and school dances. Unfortunately, for her those times were far more complicated.

The heat of the day had given way to a cool breeze. The summer sun was just now sinking below the horizon in the west in a blaze of orange. They stood silently, side by side, watching as the sky faded to pale pink, then mauve, then turned dark as velvet.

"Quite a show," Cole observed.

"God's gift at the end of the day, if you take the time to enjoy it," Cassie said.

"Do you?"

"Do I what?"

"Take the time to enjoy it? What have you been up to for the past ten years, Cassie?"

"Working."

"Doing what? Where are you living?"

Now there was the question of the hour, she thought. "I've been in a small town north of Cheyenne," she said.

"Doing?"

"The same old thing," she said, unable to hide a note of defensiveness. "Working in a diner."

"You were always good at that," he said with what sounded like genuine admiration. "You had a way of making every customer feel special, even the grumpy ones."

She shrugged. "Better tips that way."

"Why do you do that?" he asked, regarding her with a puzzled expression. "Why do you put yourself down? There's nothing wrong with being a damn fine waitress."

"No, there's not," she agreed.

He grinned. "That's better. Besides being a waitress,

what have you been up to? I imagine raising your son takes most of your time.''

She swallowed hard. Obviously he knew about Jake's existence, so there was little point in denying it. "Yes."

"I saw him, you know."

Fear made her stiffen. "You did? When?"

"The day you drove into town. I saw you go speeding past the ranch. He was with you."

She breathed a sigh of relief. Only from a distance, then. He couldn't have seen much, a glimpse at most.

"How old is he?"

"Nine."

"Then you must have had him not long after we broke up," he said, his expression thoughtful. Then, as if a dark cloud had passed in front of the sun, his eyes filled with shadows. His gaze hardened. "You didn't waste a lot of time finding somebody new, did you?"

She wanted to deny the damning conclusion to which he'd leaped, but it was safer than the alternative, safer than letting him make a connection with the timing of their relationship. "Not long," she agreed. She studied him curiously. "I didn't think it mattered what I did, since you were long gone."

"So, we're back to that," he said, his tone cold. "I wrote to you. I explained that my father insisted I go back to college right then. I asked you to wait, told you I'd get home the first chance I got."

"And I'm telling you that I never got such a letter," she said. "If I had, I would have waited." She started to add that she had loved him, but what was the point of saying that now? Whatever she had felt had died years ago.

"I would have understood," she told him, her voice flat.

"Oh, really? That wasn't how it sounded in the letter I got. You sounded as if you didn't give a rat's behind what I did."

She looked him straight in his eyes as she made another flat denial. "I never wrote to you. How could I? I didn't even know where you'd gone."

"I have the letter, dammit."

"I didn't write it," she repeated.

He studied her unflinching gaze, then sighed. "You're telling me the truth, aren't you?" He stepped away from her and raked his hand through his hair in a gesture that had become habit whenever he was troubled. "What the hell happened back then?"

Suddenly, before she could even speculate aloud, he muttered a harsh expletive. "My father, no doubt. He had something to do with it, you can be sure of that. He forced me to go, then made sure my letter never reached you. I'm sure he was responsible for the letter I got, as well."

"Wouldn't you have recognized his handwriting?"

"Of course, but he wouldn't write it himself. He'd have someone else do his dirty work."

If that was true, Cassie didn't know how she felt about it. It would be a relief to know Cole hadn't abandoned her after all, but it didn't change anything. Too much time had passed. And there was Jake to consider. Cole would be livid if he found out the boy was his.

"It doesn't matter now, Cole. It was a long time ago. We've both moved on with our lives."

He scanned her face intently. "You're happy, then?"

"Yes," she said. It was only a tiny lie. Most of the

time she was...content. At least she had been until Jake's mischief had made it necessary for her to leave the home she'd worked so hard to make for them.

"You didn't marry your son's father, though, did you?"

"No. It wouldn't have worked," she said truthfully. "Jake and I do okay on our own."

He smiled. "That's his name? Jake?"

She nodded.

"I like it."

She had known he would, because they had discussed baby names one night when they'd allowed themselves to dream about the future. Cole had evidently forgotten that, which was just as well.

"He's a good kid?"

"Most of the time," she said with a rueful grin.

"Being your son, I'll bet he's a handful. What sort of mischief does he get into?"

She found herself telling him about the computer scam, laughing now that it was behind them, admiring—despite herself—her son's audacity. "Not that I would ever in a million years tell him that. What he did was wrong. That's the only message I want him to get from me."

"We did worse," Cole pointed out.

"We certainly did not," she protested.

"We stole all the footballs right before the biggest game of the season, because I was injured and the team was likely to lose without me."

Cassie remembered. She also remembered that they'd been suspended from school for a week because of it. In high school she had loved leading the older, more popular Cole into mischief. It was only later, when he'd come home from college, that their best-buddy relationship had turned into something else.

Thinking of the stunts she'd instigated, she smiled. "That was different. No one was really harmed by it. And they played anyway. The coach went home and found a football in his garage. The team was so fired up by what we'd done, by the implication that they couldn't win without you, that they went out and won that game just to prove that they didn't need you to run one single play."

Cole laughed. "It was quite a reality check for my ego, that's for sure."

"Okay, so we chalk that one up as a stunt that backfired," she said. "Anything else you remember us doing that was so terrible?"

"There was the time you talked me into taking all the prayer books from the Episcopal church and switching them with the ones at the Baptist church." He grinned. "Why did we do that, anyway?"

She shrugged. "It seemed like a good idea at the time. And I think I was mad at my mom, because she kept pointing out prayers she thought I ought to be learning to save my soul from eternal damnation. I was tired of hearing the same ones over and over again, so I thought a switch would give her some new material."

The mention of her mother snapped her back to the present and the worries that had been stirred up about her health, first by Cole, tonight by Karen and even by that incident in town.

Suddenly she simply had to know the truth. She handed Cole her glass. "I have to go."

"Where?" he asked, his expression puzzled.

"Home. I want to talk to my mother before it gets to be too late."

The fact that he simply nodded and didn't challenge her abrupt decision to leave confirmed her fear that something must be terribly wrong. Moreover, Cole obviously knew what it was. There was too much sympathy in his expression.

"Give her my regards," he said quietly.

She considered trying to question him again about what he knew, but it was pointless. Cole could keep a secret as well as anyone, and it was evident he intended to keep this one out of loyalty to her mother.

"I will," she said.

She started across the parking lot, but he called out to her. "Cassie?"

She turned back. "Yes?"

He lifted his glass in a silent toast. "Thanks for the dance."

"Anytime," she said.

He grinned. "I'll hold you to that. There will be a great country band at the picnic tomorrow, and I haven't had a decent Texas two-step partner in years."

"You might still be saying that after tomorrow," she retorted. "I haven't been dancing in years."

And then, because she was far too tempted to go back and steal a kiss as she once would have done without a thought, she turned on her heel and strode away without another backward glance.

At home Cassie kicked off her shoes in the living room, then noted with relief that there was still a light on in her mother's room. She padded into the kitchen and brewed two cups of tea, then carried them upstairs. In her bedroom Edna was reading her Bible as she had every night before bed for as long as Cassie could remember.

"I made some tea," she announced.

Startled, her mother's gaze shot up. Worry puckered her brow. "You're home awfully early. Weren't you having a good time seeing all your friends?"

"Cole was there," she said, as if that explained everything.

"I see." Her mother set aside her Bible and patted the edge of the bed. "Come, sit beside me." She smiled. "I remember when you used to come in here after one of your dates and tell me everything you'd done."

"Almost everything," Cassie corrected dryly as she set the teacups on the nightstand and sat beside her mother.

"Some things a mother doesn't need to know."

Cassie leaned down and pressed a kiss to her mother's cheek. "I'm sorry I made things so difficult for you."

"You were testing the limits. It was natural enough. So, tell me, did you and Cole talk tonight?"

"Some, but I don't want to get into that right now." She took her mother's hand in her own, felt the calluses on the tips of her fingers put there by mending countless shirts, sewing on hundreds of buttons and hemming at least as many skirts, month after month, year after year. "I want to talk about you."

"Me?" Her mother withdrew her hand and looked away, her expression suddenly nervous. "Why would you want to talk about me?"

"Because of that spell you had in town and because twice in the past few days people have said things, things that didn't make any sense to me."

"About?"

"You." She studied her mother's face. "Are you

okay, Mom? Is there something going on that you haven't told me?''

A soft smile touched her mother's lips. She raised her hand to tuck a wayward curl behind Cassie's ear. ''I'm glad you're home for a visit.''

The evasion only made her impatient. ''Mom, tell me.''

Her mother drew in a deep breath, then blurted out, ''I have cancer.''

There it was, that single, plain-spoken word with the power to instill terror. Cassie was devastated. For a full five minutes after her mother said the words, Cassie simply stared at her in shock.

''But you don't look sick,'' she whispered finally, her voice catching on a sob. ''Except for that little spell yesterday afternoon, you've looked just fine since I got here.''

''They tell me I'm going to look a whole lot worse before they're through with me,'' her mother said, managing to inject an unexpected note of wry humor into the solemn discussion. ''And that spell was because of the heat, not the cancer.''

Tears spilled down Cassie's cheeks as she reached for the woman who'd had to endure so much by having a daughter who was always causing trouble.

''I want to know everything the doctors said. When did you find out?''

''I found the lump in my breast two weeks ago and had a needle biopsy that was positive. They wanted to operate right away, but you were coming home. I told them they'd just have to wait.''

Cassie was appalled. ''You haven't even had the surgery yet?''

"There will be time enough after you've gone back home."

"Don't be ridiculous. I'm not leaving you here to go through this alone."

"You've made a life for yourself," her mother countered. "You can't know how grateful I am that you and Jake are doing well. I won't disrupt that."

"You don't have a choice," Cassie said decisively. "We will call the doctor first thing next week and schedule the surgery. You'll need someone here when you're going through treatment, too. Will you be having radiation? Chemotherapy?"

"That will depend on what they find when they operate, but I have plenty of friends who will stand by me," her mother insisted. "I'm sure that's how Cole and Karen know. People are already rallying around with offers to drive me wherever I need to go. I don't want you turning your life upside down on my account, especially not with Cole snooping around. Who knows what sort of trouble that man and his father might stir up?"

Cassie's gaze narrowed. She had never heard her mother say a harsh word about Cole. In fact, she had always treated him as if he were her own son. Of course, if she had known all along about Cole being Jake's father, that would have colored her opinion of him.

"Cole's not important right now," Cassie said fiercely. "The only thing that matters is getting you well." Tears stung her eyes again. "Oh, Mom, you're going to beat this. I know you are."

"Yes," her mother said confidently, "I am. I intend to see my grandson grow into a fine man, one that both of us can be proud of."

"Then, no more arguments. Jake and I are staying right here with you. I'll make a quick trip to get the rest of my things, and I'll talk to Stella tomorrow about going back to work for her. If she can't take me on, I'll try the new restaurant."

"But how on earth can you keep Jake and Cole apart?" her mother asked worriedly. "I won't be responsible for Cole figuring out that the boy is his. What if he decides he wants to be a part of Jake's life? What if he asks for custody? Frank Davis will push him to, I know that much. The man is desperate for an heir for that ranch of his. It grates on his nerves that Cole only gives it half his attention."

Cassie couldn't deny that staying was a risk, but weighed against the prospect of her mother battling cancer all alone, she had no choice. "Mom, I want to be here. I owe you. You were always there for me when I needed you, even when I didn't deserve it. You are not going to face this ordeal without your family standing beside you, and that's that."

Just that easily—just that heartbreakingly—the decision to stay was made, and this time it was irreversible. Only time would tell if she would be able to live with the consequences.

Chapter Six

When Cassie finally left her mother's room, it was almost midnight. As she went to take their untouched, full teacups into the kitchen, she thought she noticed a movement on the front porch. She set the cups on a table in the foyer, slipped quietly up to the door, flipped on the overhead light and saw Cole sitting in the swing, idly setting it in motion. She wasn't nearly as surprised by his presence as she should have been, nor as dismayed.

She stepped outside, closing the door behind her. "What are you doing here?" she asked, aware that her voice was ragged and her eyes red rimmed from crying.

He turned to face her, his expression sympathetic. "I thought you might need a friendly shoulder."

"I could use one," she agreed. But his? How could she possibly turn to him? How could she let him back into her life at all?

He patted the swing. "Come on over here and tell me how your talk with your mom went."

At the moment she needed comfort more than she needed to maintain a safe emotional distance from this man who represented such a huge threat to her and her son. She sat beside him, careful to keep as much physical distance between them as the swing allowed. Cole was having none of that, though. He slid closer and draped his arm around her shoulders as he had dozens of times in the past.

She turned and met his gaze. "How did you know? I'm sure she didn't share it with you."

"It's a small town. Word gets around, especially about something like this. There have been prayers at church. Everyone wants to help out. How's she doing?"

"Better than I am," Cassie said honestly. "She thought she'd just postpone the surgery until after I was gone and I'd never have to know a thing. She didn't want me worrying. Well, she was right about one thing—I am worried. I'm scared silly, in fact."

Cole simply let her talk, his silence giving her permission to voice all of the fears she hadn't been able to express to her mother.

"I know all the statistics, but I always thought breast cancer was something that happened to other people, not to me, not to my mom. It's not just the surgery. These days they treat cancer aggressively—she's likely to have both radiation and chemo. She'll lose her hair, more than likely. She'll be exhausted. She doesn't have any kind of medical insurance. And she thought she could go through all of this alone, that she could manage. What does that say about our relationship? She's sick, really sick, and she didn't think she could count on me.''

''I don't think it was that,'' Cole said. ''Your mom's always had to be strong to face the adversities in her life. She's always had to rely on herself. She simply figured she'd deal with this the same way.''

Cassie turned her tear-filled gaze on him. ''But, Cole, she could *die*.''

Cole's expression suddenly turned bleak. ''Breast cancer survival rates are better these days than they used to be,'' he said stiffly.

Only then did she remember that Cole had lost his own mother to breast cancer years ago. She cursed herself for her insensitivity. How could she have forgotten that he'd been little more than a boy when he'd had to face what she was facing now? How much more terrifying it must have seemed to him. And his father, with all his power, hadn't been able to change the outcome. Nor had he ever gotten over the loss.

She touched a hand to his cheek. ''I'm sorry. I should have thought. You shouldn't have to listen to me go on and on about this. It's bound to bring up a lot of very painful memories.''

''Stop it,'' he said, clasping her hand in his. ''I'm the one who came over here, remember? Nobody understands better than I do what you're going through, but I'll say it again, the odds are in her favor. And stop worrying about the expense. Just put it out of your mind. I don't cared who she's seen already, we'll see to it that she has the best surgeon and the best oncologist around.''

''We?'' she echoed.

''Of course I'm going to help.''

"But why would you do that?" she asked, genuinely bewildered by the offer.

"Because she's your mother," he said simply. "Besides, for a time she was the closest thing I had to a mother, too. It hurt to lose her, when I lost you. I don't want either of us to lose her forever."

"Oh, God," Cassie whispered as the panic rose inside her again. "We're not going to, are we?"

"Not if I can help it," Cole said with grim determination.

Cassie felt some of the tension leave her body. It was as good as a promise, and at one time she had trusted Cole's promises with total confidence.

There might be a million things left for them to work out where the past was concerned, but just for tonight she wanted to believe in him again. Because he was all that stood between her and despair.

He shouldn't have promised Cassie that her mother would live. Cole paced his office, portable phone in hand, as he waited for yet another so-called expert—men who were recommended by friends—to deliver an opinion about Edna Collins's chances of survival. He'd spent the day looking for guarantees, but so far none had been given.

He told himself he was doing it as a courtesy to a woman who'd once been kind to him, but he knew better. He was doing it for Cassie. He'd recognized that bleak expression on her face, that panic she hadn't been able to keep out of her eyes. He'd seen it reflected time and again in the mirror years ago.

While his father had ranted at the doctors and cursed God, it had been left to Cole to pray, to sit and hold his mother's increasingly frail hand as she slipped farther and farther away from them. No matter that Cassie was older than he'd been, no matter what he thought of her, he didn't want her to go through that, not if he could help it.

"Why are you mixed up in this?" his father asked, his gaze speculative. "Edna Collins won't take kindly to your interference."

"What would you know about Edna Collins? You always looked down on her."

"I did not. She's a fine woman. I just thought her daughter wasn't the right woman for you—not back then, anyway."

"And now?"

"Now I'm maintaining an open mind."

"Not likely," Cole muttered. "But whatever your agenda is, Dad, keep it to yourself. Cassie and I were over and done a long time ago, and you know precisely why that is. You did your damage, and it's too late to fix things."

He needed to convince his father of that, if only to keep him from meddling and ruining whatever chance Cole might have to patch things up. This time no one would have an opportunity to interfere.

"It's never too late as long as there's breath in your body," his father said fiercely, clearly undaunted by Cole's remark. "If there's a second chance for the two of you, don't be bullheaded and waste it."

Was there a second chance? Cole wasn't certain yet. A part of him wanted there to be. To be sure all of the old feelings—that quick slam of desire—were as powerful as they'd ever been, stronger, in fact, now that they were a man's, not a boy's.

Funny how at twenty he'd thought he was so mature, so grown-up. Yet he'd let himself be manipulated and controlled. He'd given up one thing he wanted for another, never asking if the price was too high. Only later, when he'd realized Cassie was gone for good, did he consider the cost.

And then it had been too late.

The Calamity Janes had spread a half dozen quilts across the grass. Each of them had brought a cooler filled with drinks, sandwiches and a variety of desserts. There was more than enough food for themselves and most of their class, but none of them had eaten a bite.

"I can't believe it," Gina said. "Your mom was always such a skinny little thing. She looked as if a strong wind would blow her away, but she had this unmistakable strength."

"And that's exactly what's going to get her through this," Karen said, giving Cassie's hand a squeeze as she shot a warning glance at Gina. "No more talk of gloom and doom. I'm so glad you're going to stay to help out. I know how much that must mean to your mom."

"She fought me on it," Cassie admitted.

"And we all know why that was," Lauren chimed in. "Sweetie, I know you feel you need to be here, but let's think about this. What about Jake and Cole?"

"I'll just have to do whatever I can to keep them apart," Cassie said. It was going to be more easily said than done, given Cole's determination to help out with her mom's treatment in any way he could. She doubted that meant merely writing a check and steering clear of the house or whatever hospital she went to.

"You'd barely been in town for a day, and they almost ran into each other," Gina reminded her. "How can you help your mom if you're worried every second about Cole figuring out that Jake is his?''

"I think she should just tell Cole and get it over with," Karen said.

"Tell Cole what?" the very man in question inquired, making Cassie's heart thump wildly.

"Where did you come from?" she asked irritably. "You shouldn't sneak up on people when they're having private conversations."

"If you don't want anyone to overhear, then you shouldn't be having a private conversation in the middle of an event in a public park," he retorted mildly. He sat down beside her, deliberately crowding her, deliberately ignoring her scowl.

Her friends exchanged knowing looks, then one by one excused themselves to play badminton or horseshoes or baseball. Even Lauren, who'd never had an athletic bone in her body except when it came to horses, declared a sudden urge to join the women's baseball team being formed to challenge the men.

When they were all gone, Cassie looked Cole squarely in the eye. "Don't you want to play? I'm sure the men could use you."

"I'm where I want to be," he said, picking up an apple and taking a bite.

Cassie was suddenly struck by an image of Adam in the garden of Eden, tempted into sin by a seductive Eve. "Cole, you aren't imagining that you and I..." Her voice trailed off as color flooded her cheeks.

He grinned. "That we're going to have ourselves a fling for old-time's sake?"

"I wouldn't have put it like that, but yes."

"Would it be so terrible?"

"It would be a disaster," she said with feeling.

''Why? We're consenting adults now. It would be nobody's business but ours.''

She knew he probably wasn't even serious, that he was deliberately baiting her, but she couldn't let it pass. ''Do you actually think that would stop anyone from making it their business? You're the one who said it last night. This is still a small town. People love to talk. Just seeing us sitting here together now will raise eyebrows. It won't be five minutes before someone makes a call to your father to report the latest.''

He seemed totally unconcerned. ''Let them. My father doesn't run my life.''

''Since when?''

''A lot's changed since the last time we were together,'' he said mildly. ''We'll get into it one of these days.''

''No, we won't. This is impossible.''

''Nothing's impossible if you want it badly enough.''

She frowned at him. ''My mother's already been through enough. I won't have her embarrassed by my actions ever again, especially not with everything else that's going on.''

''So it's only because of your mother that you're turning me down?'' he inquired, a glint of amusement in his eyes.

''No, of course not,'' she snapped. ''It's a bad idea all the way around.''

''Then you don't find me the least bit attractive anymore?''

She knew she could never lie convincingly enough to tell him no, so she settled for saying, ''It doesn't matter whether I do or I don't. *Nothing* is going to happen.''

He shrugged. "If you say so." An infuriating, smug smile tugged at his lips.

"I say so," she said firmly.

"That's that, then." He tossed his apple toward a nearby trash can. It went in neatly. An instant later he was on his feet, his hand held out. "Come on. If we can't have sex, we might as well play ball."

Ignoring the outrageous comment and his outstretched hand, Cassie stood up, but before she could take a single step, he snagged her wrist and held her still. His gaze locked with hers and sent her heartbeat tripping.

Before she could guess his intention, his mouth settled on hers, the touch as light as a butterfly's, as devastating as ever. The world went spinning, but when she would have reached out to steady herself, he was already stepping away, apparently satisfied that she was completely off balance.

"Interesting," he commented, as if it had been nothing more than an experiment.

Still shaken, she stared at him. "What?"

"You taste exactly the way I remembered. I guess there are some things in life we can't forget, no matter how hard we try." That odd note of regret was back in his voice again.

"Try harder," she snapped, then stalked off to the sound of his laughter.

There was just one problem with that advice, she conceded as she joined the others on the ball field. There wasn't a snowball's chance in hell that she could forget it, either. Cole's kisses were as memorable now as they had been ten years ago. Hard and demanding or soft and sweet, they had always taken her by surprise, always sent her senses reeling. Time hadn't dulled that.

Okay, she admitted, she might not be able to forget. That didn't mean she couldn't steer clear of any more stolen kisses, minimize the risk, prevent disaster from striking again. It would just take some fancy footwork and plenty of polite excuses for never spending a single second with him alone.

"You okay?" Karen asked, studying her worriedly. "You look a little flushed."

"It's hot out here," she said with an unmistakable trace of defensiveness.

"It's cloudy and barely seventy," Karen pointed out.

"Do you always have to take everything so literally?" she grumbled.

Karen grinned. "Ah, this is about Cole, then. I should have known."

"Oh, go suck an egg."

"Can't. I'm next up to bat. If you want to get in the lineup, see Emma. She's managing the team."

Despite herself, Cassie chuckled. "Why am I not surprised?" Despite the rough time they had given her, Emma had always taken charge. Now that she was a big-shot attorney, no doubt she was more of a control freak than ever.

Cassie glanced at the field and reacted with amazement when she saw that Lauren was on second base. "Lauren got a hit?"

"No," Karen said, chuckling. "The pitcher got so flustered when she started moving her hips up at the plate, he walked her. She stole second when the catcher got distracted by her moves down at first. I think she's going to be our secret weapon to win this game."

"Men are so predictable," Cassie noted.

"Even Cole? I thought he'd always kept you guessing."

"Unfortunately, he's the exception." She sighed. "I could really do without an exception in my life right now."

"My advice? Go with the flow. Let the man make up for lost time if he wants to."

"And then what? Wait for the fireworks when he discovers I've spent the past nine years keeping him from his son? I don't think so. Besides, he's offered to help with my mother's medical expenses. She'll probably pitch a fit, but I don't see that we have any other choice. I can't risk having him change his mind."

"He would never renege on that commitment, and you know it."

Cassie glanced across the field and spotted Cole. He'd taken his place at second base, but he was actually ignoring the Hollywood superstar who was standing on it.

"He's really oblivious to Lauren, isn't he?" she said to Karen, feeling ridiculously pleased.

"Because there's only one of us he's ever had eyes for. That's you, honey. Don't be so quick to dismiss the possibility of getting back together with him." Her gaze narrowed. "Unless you don't love him anymore. Is that it? Have you stopped loving Cole?"

"Honestly?"

"Of course."

She did a little soul-searching, then thought of the kiss they'd just shared and almost touched a finger to her lips. "I don't know what I feel anymore."

"Then keep an open mind and find out."

"Hey, Karen, do you intend to bat anytime today?"

Emma called out impatiently. She tapped a pen against the hastily scrawled lineup on her legal pad.

"She brought a legal pad with her to a picnic?" Cassie murmured.

"Oh, yes," Karen replied. "And her cell phone. And her day planner. I think there's an entire set of law books in the trunk of her car."

Cassie gazed at Emma with dismay. "Sweet heaven, the woman's going to have a heart attack before she hits thirty."

"I've mentioned that. I've also reminded her that she has a little girl to think about." Karen shrugged. "She stares at me as if I'm speaking Swahili."

"Karen!" Emma's tone was sharp.

"Coming!" She winked at Cassie. "If I don't get a hit, I'm dead meat."

"Yes, I can see that. I think I'll go find myself a nice shady spot and rest. All this fun you're supposedly having sounds a little too stressful for me. I can't be around Emma when she gets that manic, winner-take-all glint in her eyes."

She cast a last, lingering look at Cole, but he was busy taunting Karen, trying to distract her just as the pitcher threw the ball. Cassie laughed when Karen slammed the ball in a little blooper that sailed right past him and dropped into center field. Karen reached first base, turned to Cole and stuck out her tongue.

"Way to go," Cassie shouted, then wandered off in search of shade and a little peace and quiet to recover from the traumatic news she'd received the night before. She doubted she would actually sleep, but even a few minutes alone sounded good.

Unfortunately, it seemed as if she'd barely closed her eyes and taken a deep, relaxing breath, when noise erupted from the ball field and everyone began trailing back in search of drinks and food.

"Hey, Sleeping Beauty," Cole said, dropping down beside her.

"I wasn't asleep."

"Oh, really?" he said, his expression amused. "How many innings of ball have we played since you took off?"

Cassie glanced toward Karen, but there was no help there. She was feeding plump strawberries to her husband. "I wasn't paying attention," she finally conceded.

"Five," he said. "And you slept through every one of them. You missed my home run and Emma's tantrum when Mimi Frances failed to touch third base and was declared out."

If she had slept, it hadn't done any good. She certainly didn't feel rested. "Who won?"

"The women, of course," Lauren said haughtily, sitting down beside Cole.

"Only because you used that body of yours shamelessly to distract us," Caleb accused.

"You're married. You're not supposed to be looking at Lauren's body," Karen chided, but there was amusement dancing in her eyes.

"A man would have to be dead not to notice the way she was wiggling around," he retorted.

Lauren feigned innocence. "I did nothing of the kind. I just took my turn at bat like everyone else."

"I haven't seen hips move that much since Marilyn Monroe strutted across a screen," one of the other men said.

"Are you complaining?" Gina inquired. "Seemed to me like you were all but drooling."

"I was not," he protested.

Cole leaned down and whispered in Cassie's ear, "I have no idea what all the fuss was about."

She risked meeting his gaze and saw the twinkle in his eyes that was at odds with his pious expression. "Oh, really?"

"I only have eyes for one woman here," he insisted.

"Oh? And who would that be?"

"You."

A shiver washed over her, despite herself. "Cole, don't."

"I just want you to know where I'm coming from." His expression sobered. "There's unfinished business between us, Cassie. You know there is. I think it's about time we dealt with it."

"I can't think about that now. I can't think about you," she said fiercely, scrambling to her feet.

"Where are you going?"

"For a walk."

"I'll come with you."

"No," she said, her scowl keeping him in place.

"I'll still be here when you get back," he reminded her mildly. "And nothing will have changed."

Cassie didn't care. She needed space now. She needed time to figure out why Cole could still get to her, even when she desperately wanted him not to matter at all.

"You do whatever you want to do," she told him. "You always have."

That said, she fled, but though Cole didn't follow, he stayed right smack in the middle of her thoughts. That was okay, though, she finally concluded. Thinking about the man couldn't get her into that much trouble.

Being with him could be disastrous.

Chapter Seven

"**M**om, Grandma says there are going to be fireworks tomorrow night for the Fourth of July,'' Jake said eagerly over breakfast two days later.

The class reunion had bumped smack into the town's annual holiday festivities, so people had lingered after the weekend. Unfortunately, the one person Cassie wanted most to avoid lived right here in town. Cole wouldn't be going anywhere, not anytime soon. And unless times had changed, he would be at the fireworks. His father, always a benefactor of the event, would no doubt be grand marshal of the parade. Avoiding the two of them would be next to impossible.

"Can we go, please?'' Jake pleaded. "And there's a parade, too. There will be hot dogs and all sorts of neat stuff. Grandma told me all about it.''

Cassie cast a startled look at her mother, who shrugged.

"He asked if anything special was going on for the Fourth," she explained. "I guess I got carried away."

"Mom, can we go?" Jake begged. "The Fourth of July is my very favorite holiday."

Cassie chuckled at that. "And right before Thanksgiving you always say *that's* your favorite because you love turkey and pumpkin pie. And then there's Christmas with the tree and Santa and all the presents."

"But they're not for months and months. This is my very favorite because it happens *now*. We've gotta go. Maybe I'll meet some other kids. If we're gonna be here even for a little while, I've gotta have friends."

Cassie hated the thought of denying him, but what about Cole? How could she manage to keep them apart? Or was it simply time to get used to the idea that she couldn't, not and stay here in Winding River?

"Give me a little time to think about it," she said, praying she could come up with a reasonable solution that would balance Jake's needs and her fears.

Jake's face fell. "You're going to say no, aren't you? You never want me to have any fun. You're still mad about what happened before we left home. You said when we came here I wouldn't be grounded anymore, but I might as well be if I can't do anything and I don't have one single friend to play with."

"Sweetie, it's not that," Cassie told him. "I swear it. I would love to take you. And I do want you to get to know the other kids in town." She thought desperately, trying to come up with a believable excuse for her hesitation. She could hardly tell him the truth—that she didn't want him anywhere near his father.

"It's just that your mother knows I haven't been feeling all that well," Edna broke in, throwing Cassie a lifeline. "It might have to be a last-minute decision."

Worry immediately creased Jake's brow. "You're sick?" he asked, wide-eyed.

"Nothing serious," Edna insisted, keeping to her agreement with Cassie to keep the truth from Jake for as long as possible. She fell back on the incident he had seen for himself. "But the heat bothers me some. You saw that in town the other day."

He scrambled off his chair and snuggled close to her side. "I'm sorry. We don't have to go," he said bravely, though his chin quivered ever so slightly as he made the concession.

His grandmother gave him a fierce hug. "You are such a thoughtful child. Thank you. Now why don't you go on out to the garage and see if you can get that old bike in shape to ride. Once you've got some wheels, you'll be able to get around and meet those kids." She gave him one last squeeze. "Now, go on."

Jake gave her one last worried look, then left.

"Thank you for bailing me out," Cassie said, breathing a sigh of relief when he'd gone.

"It was my fault he got his heart set on it in the first place. I just remembered how you used to love the parade and the hot dogs and the fireworks, and the next thing I knew I was feeling nostalgic and telling him all about it."

"I wish I could take him," Cassie said wistfully.

"Then do it," her mother said staunchly. "Maybe we've been going about this all wrong, keeping him from Cole. If you're determined to stay here, you can't keep Jake locked up in this house. He shouldn't be punished because of something that's not his fault."

Cassie had been thinking the same thing herself just moments earlier, but the fear the idea stirred was tough to conquer. "You know all hell will break loose if Cole adds two and two together and figures everything out."

"It might," her mother conceded. "But that child needs a father. He could do worse than Cole." Her mother seemed to be oblivious to the fact that her attitude was a major turnaround.

"That's quite a change of heart," Cassie noted.

"Not really," her mother denied, looking guilty.

"Oh? You'll have to explain that to me."

"I always thought he was a fine young man. What you told me after he left the other night, that he's willing to pay my medical expenses is proof of that. Back then I just thought things got a little out of hand between the two of you, especially with you being so young. Then when he left and you turned out to be pregnant, naturally I blamed him."

"There were two of us to blame," Cassie said, finding herself taking Cole's side as well.

"Well, of course, but he was older. I thought he took advantage of you. And, then..." She shrugged and fell silent.

"Then what?"

"Nothing. It's water under the bridge now."

Before Cassie could press her, she heard a masculine voice outside. "Oh, my God," she said, leaping up. "What if that's Cole?"

"Then you go out there and act perfectly natural," her mother advised. "Anything else will make him suspicious. Until you decide you're going to admit the truth to him, you have to keep those two apart, but you have to do it as subtly as possible. He won't see what you and I see when we look at Jake, because he won't be expecting it."

Cassie knew she was right, but that didn't stop the

panic from clawing at her as she stepped outside and saw Cole bending down to help Jake tighten a bolt on the bicycle he'd retrieved from the garage. Her heart slammed to a stop at the sight, then resumed beating at a more frantic pace.

Jake looked up at her with shining eyes. "Mom, Mr. Davis is helping me fix the bike."

"I see that. Does Mr. Davis actually have any idea what he's doing?"

Cole frowned up at her with feigned indignation. "Hey, lady, are you questioning my mechanical skills?"

She forced a grin. "You bet. I seem to recall an electric coffeepot that blew up after you'd tinkered with it."

Cole tapped the wrench against the bike. "No electricity involved here, just nuts and bolts and chains."

"True, but I'm sure you didn't stop by to do bike repair," she said. "I'll help Jake later."

"But, Mom," Jake wailed.

"I said I'd help later. Cole, why don't you come on inside? I know Mother is anxious to thank you for what you're doing for her."

"Is she really?" Cole asked, his expression skeptical.

Cassie did grin at that. "Well, she will thank you right after she tells you how she can't accept, that Edna Collins doesn't accept anyone's charity, et cetera, et cetera."

Cole got to his feet. "Now that sounds more like it. I guess I'll just have to dust off my charm."

That ought to do it, Cassie thought as he held out his hand to her son for a grown-up handshake. Certainly one member of the Collins family was under his spell. Okay, two, she conceded reluctantly. She might not hold out any hope for their future, but that didn't stop her from indulging in the occasional fantasy, the one in which she, Jake and Cole somehow put aside all the lies and deceit of the past and became a happy family.

As soon as Cole left and she could get away, Cassie invited her mother to come into town with her and Jake to have lunch at Stella's. Eager for an outing of any kind, Jake had already raced ahead to the car.

"I need to talk to Stella about that job," she explained to her mother. "This is as good a time as any. And maybe it will pacify Jake. He's still smarting over the fact that I didn't let Cole spend the whole morning helping him with that bike."

"Then you're determined to stay?" her mother asked. "Even with Cole showing up here earlier and sending you into a tizzy?"

Cassie couldn't deny that she'd been thrown, but a promise was a promise. "I told you I would. Besides, there is nowhere else I could be right now. You need me."

Her mother nodded, and what might have been relief passed across her face. "That's that, then," she said giving Cassie's hand a squeeze. "It'll be good to have the two of you here. The house gets awfully quiet sometimes."

"I thought you'd be grateful for that after all the ruckus I raised as a kid."

Her mother smiled. "I was for a time, but no more. Having Jake running in and out, having you to talk to now that you're a grown-up woman yourself, it's a real blessing, Cassie. I'm grateful."

"I don't need your gratitude, Mom. I belong here, especially now. Go on and get your purse. I'm going to buy you the biggest sundae Stella can make."

"Oh, my, I couldn't possibly," her mother said, but she looked tempted as she followed Cassie to the car.

"Of course you can," Cassie said as she checked to make sure everyone had fastened their seat belts. Then she grinned at her mother. "And you can have it before lunch."

Her mother looked horrified. "Heavens, no. It will ruin my appetite."

"So what?" Cassie said as they made the quick trip to Main Street. "Why can't we have dessert first every now and again on a special occasion?"

"And what occasion would that be?" her mother asked as Cassie pulled into a parking spot in front of the diner.

"My homecoming, of course."

A rare and full-fledged smile spread across her mother's too-pale face. "Now that really is worth celebrating."

She said it with such genuine emotion that Cassie had to blink back tears. Maybe she'd had it wrong all these years. Maybe her mother really had missed her.

"Can I celebrate, too?" Jake asked from the back.

"Absolutely," Cassie agreed.

"And we're really going to stay here?" he asked. "You're not going to change your mind again?"

"I'm not changing my mind," Cassie said firmly.

He pumped a fist into the air. "All right!"

When they were settled into a booth at Stella's, Cassie beckoned her old boss over. "We need three large sundaes, two hot fudge." She glanced at her mother. "Caramel or strawberry?"

"Definitely strawberry," her mother said.

Stella reacted with shock. "No main course? Not even a burger?"

"Not yet," Cassie said.

"Anything else?"

"How about a job?"

Stella's mouth gaped. She stuck her order pad in her pocket, then scooted into the booth next to Cassie. "You're looking for work?"

Cassie nodded.

"Well, hallelujah! That must mean you're home to stay."

"I am."

"Then you can start tomorrow. With the parade and all, it's going to be a zoo in here, and the teenage girl I had working for me announced today that she intended to spend the Fourth with her boyfriend whether I liked it or not."

"Did you fire her?"

Stella chuckled. "I will now. Irresponsible kids need to be taught a lesson." She patted Cassie's hand. "Didn't take long for you to catch on, did it? One warning had you in here right on time every single day you were scheduled."

"I liked the perks," Cassie said with a grin. "All the ice cream I could eat."

"It was a small price to pay for a reliable worker," Stella replied.

After she'd gone off to fix their sundaes, Jake left his grandmother's side to squeeze in next to Cassie. "If we're gonna stay, that means I can spend more time with Mr. Davis, doesn't it? My friends back home will be so jealous when I tell them I know him. I mean, he's almost like a celebrity."

"In that case you should understand that you can't go bothering him. I'm sure he has lots and lots of work to do," Cassie said.

"But I asked him if he would explain to me about computers and how they work and stuff, and he said he would." Jake regarded her with an earnest, hopeful expression. "He said he wouldn't mind at all."

Cassie exchanged a helpless look with her mother. Leave it to Jake to take matters into his own hands.

"We'll see," Cassie said evasively.

"I think we should go after lunch, before he forgets," Jake said.

"No, not today," Cassie told him firmly.

"When?"

"I'll talk to him and work something out," she said, grateful when Stella appeared with their sundaes.

The ice cream distracted Jake for maybe five minutes before he began to badger her again.

"If you don't drop this right now," Cassie said finally, "you won't see him at all."

"But—"

"I said to drop it."

Tears welled up in Jake's eyes, but he fell silent, shoving the rest of his sundae away in protest. Cassie's appetite disappeared, as well. Only her mother continued to enjoy her sundae, or at least pretended to.

Was this what it was going to be like living in Winding River, a constant tug-of-war with her son over his hero worship of a man he didn't even realize was his father?

By the time they left for home, Cassie had a splitting headache and a knot the size of Wyoming in her stomach. At this rate she was going to wind up in a hospital bed right next to her mother's.

* * *

Naturally Jake didn't take her decision as final. Nor did the concession she made, allowing him to attend the parade and fireworks, appease him. She had to admit that had gone well enough. If Cole had been around, she hadn't spotted him. And Jake's delight had been worth every second of nervousness she'd experienced.

But by the next morning the treat had been forgotten, and Jake was back on the subject of going to see Cole. Her repeated warnings that she didn't want to hear another word about it seemed to fall on deaf ears.

He continued to pester her for the rest of the week about going out to the Double D. He'd gotten his stubbornness and willfulness from her, no doubt about it.

She steadfastly continued to refuse to take him to visit Cole, making up excuse after excuse, but Cassie could see that they were wearing thin. Even so, she was stunned when Jake disappeared on Saturday morning. She searched high and low, but finally had to admit there was no sign of him.

"Mom, have you seen Jake?"

"Not since breakfast. Why?"

"He's not in the house. He's not working on the bike, and nobody on the block has seen him. I've looked everywhere I can think of."

"You don't suppose he's gone out to Cole's ranch, do you?" Edna asked, as aware as Cassie of her grandson's obsession.

That was exactly what Cassie feared. "How would he get there, though?"

"I imagine it wouldn't be all that difficult to get somebody to give him a lift. Half the ranchers in town on a Saturday take that road back home. All the boy would have to do is ask one of them."

"Should I call out there?"

"Why not ride around town first and see if anyone's seen him," her mother suggested. "No point in getting Cole involved if the boy's just wandered off to get an ice cream cone or something."

But no one in town had seen Jake. Cassie was about to reach for the phone to call Cole when it rang.

"You looking for Jake, by any chance?" Cole asked without preamble.

"Oh, my God," Cassie murmured. "He *is* with you. Is he okay?"

"He looks fine to me, but I thought you might be worried. He was pretty evasive at first when I asked how he got here and whether he had your permission to come. I got the feeling he didn't tell you before he hitchhiked out here."

"He *what?*"

"Pete gave him a ride on his way back from Stella's," Cole explained. Then he assured her, "He's okay, Cassie."

"That's not the point. I'm going to wring his scrawny little neck. I'll be there in twenty minutes."

"Take your time and cool off a little. Keep reminding yourself that there's been no harm done."

"Don't tell me what to do where my son's concerned," she snapped, and slammed down the phone.

"He's with Cole?" her mother asked.

"Oh, yes."

"Should I come with you?"

She shook her head. "No. Cole was right about one thing. I do need to calm down before I get out there. No telling what I might say."

Cassie made it to the Double D in less than the twenty minutes it usually took. The front door was standing open as if she were expected, so she went straight in. Oblivious to the grandeur of the antiques that generations of Davises had collected over the years, she went in search of her son.

When she finally found the two of them in Cole's office, heads bent over the computer keyboard, her blood ran cold. Jake looked happier than she'd seen him in ages. Just thinking about the bond the two of them were obviously forming made her knees go weak. She had to lean against the doorjamb for support.

"Look right natural together, don't they?" Frank Davis remarked, slipping up quietly to stand at her shoulder in the doorway.

Something in his voice alerted her. She stepped away from the room and turned to study the man who had probably come between her and Cole.

Frank Davis had a powerful build. His shock of dark-brown hair was streaked with gray now, but there was still plenty of spark in his blue eyes, and he wore that same arrogant, superior expression that had intimidated her as a girl. Oddly she discovered that he didn't scare her now. She met his gaze without flinching.

"What are you saying?" she asked in a cool, deliberate tone.

Her reaction seemed to amuse him. "I'm saying I know."

"Know what?"

He smirked. "One look is all it takes to know that boy is my grandson. Even if your mama hadn't told me the truth years ago, I would have seen it right off."

Despite her determination not to let the man get to her, Cassie felt faint for the second time in just a few minutes. This time she had to will herself not to lean against the wall for support.

"My mother told you?" Her mother had never said a single word to Cassie about her suspicions, but she had discussed them with Cole's father? What had she been thinking?

"She thought I had a right to know."

More likely her mother had been desperate for advice from the one person she'd assumed had as big a stake in keeping the secret as she did. Oh, Mom, what have you done? Cassie thought as she stared into that confident gaze. And why didn't you warn me?

"Does Cole know?"

"Not unless he's figured it out in the last half hour."

"Why haven't you told him?" Understanding dawned. "You haven't hold him because even now you don't think I'm good enough for him, because you don't want him to know that I had his child. You're afraid he'll insist on marrying me. That's why you came between us years ago, sending him back to school, then getting someone to write him a note saying I was breaking it off for good. That was you, wasn't it?"

Color rose in Frank's cheeks, but he didn't deny the accusation. "You two were way too young to get involved. Your mother and I did what we thought was best."

His words delivered yet another blow. The two of them had conspired, even before they had known about the pregnancy? She felt as if she were standing on a slippery slope and beginning to skid. Nothing seemed certain anymore.

"My mother?" she repeated, needing to understand,

praying she was mistaken. "What did she have to do with it?"

"Who do you think wrote the note that Cole got? And who kept his note from you? No way I could keep Berta Smith from delivering it. She takes her duties at the post office real serious. But your mama got it out of the box and ripped it up."

"Oh, my God," she whispered, brokenhearted at the thought of the betrayal that had changed not just her life and Cole's but their son's, as well. Maybe they wouldn't have married if Cole had known about the pregnancy, but they'd never had a chance to decide things for themselves. Each had been convinced of the other's betrayal. As a result the choices had been taken out of their hands.

"Well, the lies are over now," Frank said, a complacent expression settling on his face. "Cole will know about his son soon enough, and if I know my boy, he'll be furious that you kept such a secret from him. He'll fight you for custody."

Cassie felt sick to her stomach as she realized that even now the man was scheming against her. "That's what you're counting on, isn't it? That he'll reject me but claim Jake?"

His eyes glittered with satisfaction. "That's exactly right. You won't stand a chance of keeping the boy, not in this state."

If she hadn't been filled with such white-hot fury, Cassie might have been chilled by his threat or by the triumphant expression on his face. Instead, poking him in the chest, she backed him up against the opposite wall, oblivious to the difference in their sizes, oblivious to anything beyond the outrage that his smug remark had stirred.

"You will never take my boy from me," she said in a low tone, praying it wouldn't carry down the hall. "Never. Not if I have to see you in hell first."

She must not have gotten the right note of warning in her voice, because she could still hear Frank's chuckle echoing after her as she stormed into Cole's office to claim her son.

Chapter Eight

Cole had heard Cassie's raised voice in the hall but couldn't imagine what she and his father had to fight about, especially since his father had been giving so much lip service lately to the prospect of Cole getting back together with her.

Then their voices had dropped, and he hadn't given the subject much thought since the boy sitting beside him was hurling questions at him so fast his head was spinning. The kid clearly had an insatiable curiosity when it came to computers, and he was smart, too. Cole didn't have to talk down to him. Given what Cassie had told him about the trouble Jake had gotten into on a computer, he probably shouldn't have been surprised, but he was.

When he finally glanced up from the screen and spotted Cassie, his pulse took another one of those wicked lurches. She was wearing a sundress that showed off the satiny skin of her shoulders and her long, shapely calves. Her cheeks were flushed with color and her eyes sparkled dangerously. Whatever she and Frank had been discussing, it had rankled.

"Jake Collins!" she said sternly, avoiding Cole's gaze altogether.

The boy glanced up at Cole, then gave a resigned shrug. "Yes, ma'am."

"Do you have any idea at all how much trouble you're in?"

"A lot?" he said hesitantly.

"Oh, yes," she said. "You know you are not supposed to be here, that you are not supposed to hitch rides with strangers and that you are always supposed to tell me where you're going."

"You wouldn't let me come," Jake said, as if that were excuse enough.

"I had my reasons," she said direly. "And that's all that matters. You disobeyed me, and I won't have it. Am I getting through to you yet?"

Cole saw Jake's shoulders slump and immediately felt sorry for the kid. He knew what the boy had done was wrong, but no harm had come out of it. Shouldn't Cassie be thankful for that, at least? Ignoring the temper flashing in her eyes, he decided he'd better intercede.

"He's already assured me that nothing like this will ever happen again," he said, gazing directly at the boy. "Right, Jake?"

Clearly sensing a powerful ally, Jake nodded eagerly. "I'll get permission next time."

"Not likely," Cassie muttered. She leveled a stern look at Jake. "There will not be a next time, period. End of discussion."

Cole stared at her, curious about what had infuriated her so much. Was it Jake's disobedience? Panic over what could have happened to a kid out hitchhiking, even in this relatively safe community?

Or did it specifically have to do with him? This was the second time he'd gotten the feeling she didn't want him spending time with her son.

There could be any number of reasons for that, of course. A lot of responsible single mothers tried to keep some distance between their children and the men in their lives, at least until they knew if the relationship was going to lead somewhere. That didn't seem to apply here, since he and Cassie weren't exactly having a relationship and she'd stated quite clearly that she didn't intend for that to change.

Maybe it was just a case of protecting the boy from being disappointed by a man who had disappointed her in the past.

Still trying to figure it out, Cole gave her a penetrating look, but her face was giving away nothing. Because he found that annoying, he deliberately set out to provoke an honest answer out of her.

"What was that you said, Cassie?" he taunted mildly. "Something about there not being a next time?"

She gave him a sweet, completely insincere smile. "That's right. Jake knows he shouldn't be bothering you."

"I don't mind."

"Well, I do," she said, her look meant as a warning that he wasn't to contradict her. "We have to leave now. Jake, go to the car. I'll be there in a minute. Cole and I have a few things we need to clear up."

Cole could hardly wait to hear what those were.

"But, Mom—"

"Go," she repeated in a way that had her son scrambling from the chair.

Jake skidded to a stop as he reached the door. "Bye, Cole. Thanks."

"Anytime," he said, deliberately defying Cassie, his gaze locked with hers.

There was no mistaking the storm brewing in her eyes. He felt a rare spark of anticipation. He'd been itching to get into a good old-fashioned, rip-roaring fight with her for days now. It was the only time she let down those rock-solid defenses of hers. This seemed as good a battle as any, especially since she appeared as eager as he was to start it.

The minute Jake was out of sight, Cassie marched up to the desk, then leaned down until her face was just inches above his. The effect was ruined somewhat by the way her sundress gaped, but she was clearly oblivious to that. She would have been appalled had she known.

"I will not have my son out here, do you understand me?" she snapped. "Where he goes and what he does are my decisions."

"You are his mother," he agreed.

She scowled at him, then added, "He is *my* son and *my* responsibility."

"No question about that," he said, then locked gazes with her. "Where's his father? How much say does he have in things?" He'd let that issue pass once before, but he'd concluded it was time to get it out in the open.

Dismay flickered briefly in her eyes, then vanished. "None of your business. All you need to know is that when it comes to Jake, I make the rules." She shook her head, regarding him with evident distaste. "I can't understand how I overlooked this years ago. You Davis men are all alike.''

He stared at her, startled by the very real venom in her voice. Clearly he'd missed something. "What the hell does that mean?" he demanded. "Does this have something to do with the argument you and my father were having out there in the hall?"

Something that might have been panic registered in her expression for just an instant, long enough to betray the fact that she wasn't nearly as calm as she pretended to be when she shrugged. Then that cool mask he'd come to hate slid back into place.

"Just a difference of opinion," she said mildly.

"About?"

"I don't want to get into it now."

"I do."

"Then this will be just one more instance in life when you don't get what you want. Get used to it," she said.

The woman had developed a lot of spunk over the years; he had to give her that. Back when they'd been dating, she had been all brash bravado. Few people had ever seen past it to the vulnerable girl inside. Cole had. Now, though, her feistiness ran deeper, carried more conviction and self-confidence.

Still, he couldn't seem to shake the memory of that tiny, fleeting glimpse of fear he'd caught earlier.

"I'm sorry if my father said something to upset you," he offered, treading carefully, still hoping to get an honest explanation.

"He didn't," she insisted. "Your father doesn't scare me. He never has."

"But he tried to," Cole guessed. What he couldn't understand was why his father would do such a thing.

For days now he'd been doing everything in his power to bring the two of them together. Was he just trying a different tactic with Cassie? Maybe a little reverse psychology, since his blatant scheming obviously hadn't worked on Cole?

"I have to go," Cassie said, ignoring his question. "I need to get out there to Jake before he gets it into his head to hitchhike back home."

"I imagine my father's keeping him company."

The color drained out of her face at that. "All the more reason for me to go. I don't want him influencing Jake in any way."

"Are you suggesting he did a lousy job with me?" Cole said.

She shrugged. "If the shoe fits..." Her expression turned intense. "I meant what I said earlier, Cole, I don't want Jake out here. And I don't want you encouraging him to come. Are we clear about that?"

Her implication—that he and his father were somehow lousy role models for her son—grated. Added to the heat and tension that swirled in the air every time he and Cassie got together, it was more than Cole could take. He was overcome by a need to do something about it, to rattle her so badly she would lose that distant, disdainful expression.

Before he could consider the ramifications, he reached out and hauled her into his lap and settled his mouth over hers, muffling her gasp of protest.

She tasted of cinnamon and maybe a lingering hint of mint. Her lips were as soft as he'd remembered, if not nearly as willing as they had been even the other day at the picnic. She struggled in his arms, bit down on his lower lip. He winced at the taste of blood, became more determined than ever to tame her, to remind her of the way she had once melted in his arms.

He framed her face with his hands, looked long and deep into her flashing eyes, waited for the anger to die, then slanted his mouth over hers once more.

This time she shuddered, then relaxed in his embrace before kissing him back. Temper gave way to passion, chilly disdain turned to fiery acceptance.

They were both breathless and panting when he finally released her with a great deal of reluctance. She stared back at him with dazed eyes. Slowly her gaze cleared and the temper came roaring back. It was like watching water come to a boil, simmering slowly at first, then suddenly bubbling up and over.

"Damn you," she murmured, then shot to her feet. "I won't let you do this to me, not again."

She whirled around and stalked from the room without another word. A smile crept across Cole's face as he watched her go.

"When it comes to you, Cassie, and most of those rules you're so intent on reminding me of," he said softly, "they were made to be broken."

"And then he kissed me," Cassie told Gina, all but quivering with outrage. "Can you imagine?"

"The man's a cad," Gina agreed, barely containing a grin.

"Are you laughing at me?"

"Never," Gina denied, though her smile spread.

"You *are* laughing at me."

"It's just that the whole time you're trying to sound so outraged, there's a very becoming blush on your cheeks."

"Because I'm furious."

"Why? Because he kissed you or because you liked it?"

"I did not like it," Cassie said emphatically.

Gina looked skeptical. "He's lost his touch?"

"I never said that. It's not important whether or not he's a good kisser. The point is that he had no business kissing me in the first place. We were fighting. It was a sneaky, low-down way to make me forget that."

"He wants you back," Gina said.

"Don't be crazy. He doesn't want me back any more than I want him."

"If you say so."

Cassie scowled. "I do," she said, even though her conviction was weakening.

"Okay, then. There's nothing to worry about. You're not going to be swayed by a few harmless little kisses, then, are you?"

There had been nothing harmless about those kisses. They had been devastating, Cassie admitted to herself. She could deny it to her friend from now till doomsday and it wouldn't change the truth. She sighed. Everything was so blasted complicated.

"Let's forget about Cole," she said.

"Okay by me."

"I want to hear about you. Who is that handsome man you were with over the weekend? I've never seen him before. Is he a friend from New York?"

Gina suddenly looked uncomfortable. "I have no idea who you mean."

"The man who was following you around like he'd never met such an exotic creature before."

"Oh, him," Gina said, then shrugged. "He's a nuisance. Nothing more. He's probably gone by now."

"I don't think so," Cassie said, glancing pointedly

outside, where the very man under discussion was lurking on the sidewalk.

Gina followed the direction of her gaze, then sighed heavily, her expression miserable. "Well, hell," she muttered under her breath.

Cassie studied her intently, saw the genuine worry in her friend's eyes. "Gina, what's really going on? Who is he?"

"Nobody important," her friend said staunchly, but she slid out of the booth. She gave Cassie a hug. "See you later. If you ask me, you ought to consider what Cole's offering."

The comment was enough to throw Cassie and keep her from asking all the other questions on the tip of her tongue as Gina left Stella's. She watched idly as Gina marched up to the man, appeared to exchange words with him, then took off alone in the direction of her car. Another example of true love not running smoothly, perhaps?

And speaking of that, what the heck had Gina meant with that comment about taking what Cole was offering? As far as Cassie could see, he wasn't offering a blessed thing. A few stolen kisses didn't add up to anything...except maybe trouble. And frankly she had more of that in her life these days than she could possibly cope with.

Dismissing that and Gina's odd behavior, she went back to work. Stella's was as busy as ever at lunchtime. Cassie was on the run until almost two.

"Go," Stella said, taking her last order from her. "I know you have to get your mother to the hospital. And I don't want to see you anywhere near here in the morning. I can manage. You stay right there until she's out of surgery and you know how she's doing."

"Thank you, Stella. You're an angel."

"Good heavens, don't be spreading that around," the older woman pleaded. "The only way I keep my customers in line is having them think I'm a tyrant."

Cassie laughed. "I hate to tell you this, but you don't have anyone in town fooled."

Stella looked genuinely disappointed. "Well, shucks. I guess I'm just going to have to work a little harder at it. Now, scoot."

"Hey, how about getting that burger over here before I starve to death?" Hank Folsom hollered.

"Keep your britches on, Hank," Stella shouted right back. "If you don't like the service in here, you can just march right through the door and get your lunch someplace else." She winked at Cassie. "How was that?"

"Tough as nails," Cassie assured her. "Unfortunately, it's an idle threat. There is no place else in town to get a burger."

"I know," Stella said with satisfaction. "Works out real nice, don't you think?"

Cassie was still chuckling over that when she got home and found her mother sitting on the sofa in her best dress, her suitcase sitting beside her. Jake hovered nearby, looking worried. They had told him about the surgery the night before, talking about it only in the most upbeat and positive way, but it had clearly rattled him.

"I'm going to the hospital with you," Jake said, shooting a defiant look at Cassie.

"I made arrangements for you to stay next door."

"Well, I'm not going to."

"Let him come," her mother said. "He'll just worry

if he stays here with Mildred, and he'll be company for you.''

Cassie finally relented. "Okay, give me two seconds to change and we'll head on up to Laramie to the hospital.''

The screen door banged open just then. "She's not going to Laramie," Cole said. "I've made arrangements for her to go to University Hospital down in Denver. The doctor there has consulted with her doctor. Her records were sent to him yesterday once your mother okayed it.''

Cassie's mouth dropped open. "What right did you have to do that?" Cassie demanded finally. She looked at her mother. "You knew about this?''

"I knew it was a possibility," Edna said.

Cole regarded Cassie evenly. "I told you at the beginning that I was going to see that she had the best care possible. We're going to Denver. I've got my plane all fueled up.''

Jake's eyes widened, oblivious to anything except Cole's announcement. "We're going in a real plane? One of those ones I saw at the airport on the way into town?''

Cole grinned at his enthusiasm. "That's right. If you're good, I'll even let you take the controls for a minute.''

"Over my dead body," Cassie said at once.

Before that could erupt into a full-fledged battle, her mother said quietly, "I think if Cole's gone to all this trouble, then we should do as he says. We're certainly not going to drive all that way.''

Cassie stared at her. "Mom, you've always sworn you would never set foot in an airplane.''

"This is different.''

"How?"

"I'm sure Cole knows what he's doing."

"He just told a nine-year-old he could operate the controls," Cassie pointed out.

"It's not as if I'm going to nod off and take a nap while Jake flies us to Denver," Cole said mildly. "And I know you want your mother to have the very best chance she can have. The surgeon in Denver comes highly recommended."

"Why didn't you say anything about this before?" Cassie asked.

"Because he didn't have an opening in his schedule until yesterday. The minute he called me, I spoke to your mother and made the arrangements."

Cassie felt as if the entire situation, already terrifying enough, was spinning wildly out of control. It wasn't just that the four of them would be stuck in close quarters in that tiny plane, it was the fact that Cole clearly intended to be right by her side all through her mother's surgery. On the one hand the gesture was both generous and kind. On the other, it would inevitably tighten the bond between them. Worse, it would keep him and his son in close proximity for hours, if not days.

In the end, though, Cassie knew she had no choice. The only thing that mattered was getting her mother the finest treatment available. And while the doctor in Laramie was surely good, the one in Denver would have greater experience and perhaps a more experienced support staff, as well.

Swallowing her pride—and her fear—she finally nodded. "Let's go, then."

In the plane Cole was true to his word. He allowed the awestruck Jake to take over the controls, if only for a few minutes. It was an experience Cassie knew her son would never forget. By the time they landed in Denver, his case of hero worship was stronger than ever.

They checked her mother into the hospital, then saw her settled into the private room Cole had arranged. When the surgeon came in to speak to her, Cassie was impressed with his warmth, his reassurances and his detailed explanations about what her mother could expect in the morning. In his early fifties, he was clearly both experienced and compassionate. For the first time since she had learned of her mother's diagnosis, Cassie could see hope in her mother's eyes.

"He seemed like a nice man," her mother said, following the surgeon with her gaze as he left the room.

"We couldn't have found a better doctor," Cole said.

"Nice-looking, too," Cassie teased her mother. "No wonder there's a little color in your cheeks."

"Stop with that," her mother said, clearly flustered. The pink in her cheeks deepened. "All I care about is how good he is with that scalpel of his."

A few minutes later a nurse came in. "We're going to give your mother a little something to help her relax and get a good night's sleep."

"Then you all might as well run along," Edna said. "I'm in good hands." She reached for Cole's hand. "And it's all thanks to you. I don't know how I'll ever repay you."

He bent down and kissed her cheek. "All you need to do for me is get well and live a long and healthy life."

"I'm going to do my best." Her gaze locked on Cole's. "Keep an eye on my girl for me, okay?"

Cole glanced Cassie's way. "Always," he said softly.

Trying to ignore the fluttery feeling in the pit of her stomach caused by Cole's promise, Cassie gave her mother a kiss. "See you in the morning, Mom. I love you."

Now that the time had come to leave, Jake looked shaken. He edged close to the bad. "I don't want to go, Grandma."

She brushed the hair out of his eyes. "I'm going to be just fine," she reassured him. "Go with your mom and Cole. Get something good to eat and see the sights. This time tomorrow you can come back here and tell me all about them."

Jake still looked reluctant. Cole squeezed his shoulder. "Come along, son."

Even though he spoke casually, in a way men spoke to young boys all the time without it meaning a thing, Cassie froze. Hearing him call Jake *son,* no matter the context, made her tremble. How long? she wondered, exchanging a look with her mother. How long would it be before Cole realized that the boy he was addressing really was his son?

Cole did his best to relieve Cassie's tension over a quick dinner in a fast-food restaurant. He enumerated all of the surgeon's qualifications and cited all of the latest cancer recovery statistics. But nothing he said seemed to get through to her. She listened, she nodded, but her fingers continued to shred napkin after napkin until there was a pile of white fluff on the table in front of her.

Finally he reached across the table and placed his hand over hers. "Enough," he said gently. He glanced pointedly at the normally effusive Jake, who had grown increasingly silent as the meal went on, clearly picking up on her mood.

Cassie's gaze flew to her son. "Sweetie, are you okay?"

He shook his head. "I'm scared," he admitted.

"You heard Cole. Grandma's doctor is the best. She's going to get well."

Jake regarded her hopefully. "You believe that?"

"With all my heart," she said fervently.

"Then how come you're acting like you're scared, too?" He pointed to the mound of shredded napkins.

Cassie stared at them, looking vaguely startled. "Oh, dear, I guess my mind was on all sorts of things."

"What things?" Jake promptly wanted to know.

She forced a grin. "Cabbages and kings."

"Mom!"

Cole wanted to protest, as well. He'd hoped Jake might get a straight answer out of her. He doubted *he* could. If it wasn't her mother that had her looking so worried, then what could it be?

Only after they'd gone to the hotel near the hospital and settled Jake in bed did Cole get a chance to ask. He was pacing the suite's living room when Cassie finally joined him. He hadn't been at all sure that she would. He had the oddest feeling that he was the cause of her nervousness, though why that should be he couldn't imagine. And surely that kiss they'd shared hadn't rattled her so badly that she was scared to be in the same room with him. It wasn't as if he was likely to try to ravish her on the eve of her mother's surgery.

"Jake asleep?"

She nodded.

"How are you?"

"Scared, just like he said."

"About your mother?"

She shot him a startled look, then glanced away. "Of course," she said hurriedly. "What else?"

"That's what I was wondering." He studied her intently. "You're not scared of me, are you? Of being here in a hotel room with me overnight?"

A glimmer of a smile passed across her face as she gestured around the suite. "It's not as if we're in cramped quarters, Cole. We won't even be sleeping in the same room."

"More's the pity," he murmured.

She frowned at him. "Why would you say that?"

"Because it's true."

"Cole, we can't go back."

"Then how about going forward?"

She shook her head without giving the notion a moment's consideration. That grated on him more than he could say.

"You always were too blasted stubborn for your own good."

"Then I'm surprised you'd want to bother with me."

"Unfortunately, you're still the only woman who's ever fascinated me."

"Cole!"

The protest was only halfhearted, which he considered encouraging. "It's true," he said, stepping closer until he could lift his hand to her cheek. Her skin was like cool satin, but it warmed beneath his touch as if he'd stirred a fire to life below the surface. He rubbed the pad of his thumb across her lips and felt her shudder.

It took every bit of willpower he possessed not to claim her mouth and satisfy the urgency already building inside him. Not tonight, he warned himself. Taking advantage of her vulnerability was no way to win her heart. It would just give her more ammunition to use against him.

Slow and steady, he reminded himself. Like the tortoise. Winning, not speed, was the goal. In fact, in the past few weeks he'd begun to wonder how he'd ever lost sight of that goal, even for a single second.

Chapter Nine

Cassie alternated between pacing the hospital waiting room and huddling miserably in a corner, trying not to look at the other families. Each time she did, she saw her own fear reflected in their faces. It was more than she could bear.

Instead of thinking about what was going on in the operating room, she forced herself to think about Cole. He was the only distraction that stood a chance against the weight of her concern for her mother. Right now he and Jake were off on a shopping expedition, ostensibly to find something suitable for her mother.

"Just a little get-well gift," Cole had assured her. "It will keep Jake's mind off everything."

She couldn't fault him for wanting to do that for her son. In fact, there was very little she could fault him on these days. He had been nothing but kind and utterly thoughtful. It reminded her of why she'd fallen in love with him years ago.

It was driving her nuts.

Even the night before, when she had thought for sure he was going to take advantage of both proximity and her fragile emotional state, Cole had behaved like a perfect gentleman, backing off before things could get too heated.

His consideration was like a magnet. She wanted so badly to lean on him, to accept the comfort he was offering, but the past had taught her that the only person she could count on was herself. And her mother, of course.

Now, though, it was because of her mother's health that she needed someone to help her be strong. And it would be folly to let Cole be that person, even for a second.

''There she is,'' a familiar voice whispered.

Cassie's gaze shot up to see her four best friends hovering in the doorway of the waiting room. Tears stung her eyes, then rolled down her cheeks. *These* were people she could trust, women who had always been there for her. When times got tough, the Calamity Janes had always hung together.

''You guys,'' she murmured, crossing the room to be enfolded in a fierce group hug. ''What are you doing here?''

''Did you honestly think we were going to let you go through this alone?'' Karen chided.

''No way,'' Lauren declared.

She was wearing jeans and a faded blouse and hiding behind a pair of oversize sunglasses and a floppy hat, but none of that could disguise the fact that she was the glamorous one among them. Hollywood had taught her too much for her ever to be the plain Jane of the group again.

"The Calamity Janes stick together through thick and thin, remember?" she said to Cassie.

Cassie gave her a watery smile. "I remember."

"Any word yet?" Emma asked.

"Nothing. She's still in surgery."

Gina squeezed her hand. "Where's Jake?"

"With Cole."

Three pairs of eyes regarded her incredulously. Even Lauren removed her sunglasses long enough to stare.

"He volunteered to keep Jake occupied. What could I do?" Cassie asked defensively.

"Why is he even here in the first place?" Emma demanded in her best ready-to-charge-into-battle voice.

"He made the arrangements for Mom to be treated here, instead of in Laramie. In fact, come to think of it, how did you find out where we were? It all happened so fast I never even had a chance to call and let you know."

"Lauren waved her magic wand and, *poof*, information was forthcoming. Then a jet appeared. The woman has contacts," Gina said respectfully. She feigned an exaggerated bow. "I am in awe."

"One of the few perks of stardom worth having," Lauren said with a distinct edge to her voice. Then, before anyone could question her, she tucked an arm around Cassie's waist. "Come on. Let's sit down over here where we won't be the center of attention. You doing okay, sweetie?" She whipped open a bag, and cups of gourmet coffee appeared for all of them.

"Hanging in," Cassie said, taking the cup and breathing in the aroma. Hazelnut. "I thought I'd know something by now, but it seems like it's been forever and there's still no word.''

Lauren nodded and set aside her own coffee. ''Then let me see what I can find out.''

As soon as she'd gone, Emma shook her head. ''I don't know how she does it. Even incognito, she has a way of commanding respect. You should have seen her down at the information desk. The poor volunteer kept trying to tell us that only family was permitted up here, but Lauren finally persuaded her that we were as close to being family as anybody could be. She did it in a Southern voice straight out of *Gone with the Wind.* I kept looking around to see who was talking. Next thing you know we're on an elevator with a little map showing us precisely where the waiting room is located. If I could do what she does, I'd never lose a case.''

''You never lose a case, anyway,'' Karen pointed out.

Emma frowned. ''That's not true. I've lost some.''

''How many?'' Gina teased. ''One? Two?''

''Four,'' Emma retorted.

Gina rolled her eyes. ''Out of how many?''

''I don't know.''

''Hundreds, I imagine,'' Gina countered.

''The point is, Lauren is very good at what she does,'' Emma said.

''Then why does she look so unhappy?'' Cassie wondered.

''I've been asking myself the same thing,'' Karen said, her expression thoughtful. ''And I know she wanted to stick around for your mom's surgery, but she's showing no inclination at all to get back to her glamorous life in Hollywood. Every time I bring up anything about her career, she puts me off.''

"Well, it can't be because she's having trouble getting roles,'' Cassie said. "I saw on TV the other night that there are two producers who are counting on her starring in their next films.''

"Which producers? What films?'' Gina asked with the starstruck fascination of an old movie buff.

"I don't remember, but I do recall that both admitted she hasn't committed yet.''

The discussion of Lauren's apparent unhappiness ended when she came back into the waiting room with a triumphant expression and the bemused surgeon in tow.

"Look who I found,'' she announced happily. "And the news is good.'' She beamed at him. "I said that straight off, because you doctors always hem and haw before you get to the bottom line.''

He regarded her with a dazed expression. "Who are you again?''

"Just a friend of the family.''

He still looked puzzled. "But you look so familiar.''

She sighed dramatically. "See what I mean about dillydallying. Come on, Doc. Tell Cassie how her mom's surgery went.''

He gathered his composure and faced Cassie. "Everything went exactly as I'd hoped it would. The cancer appeared to be contained. We did a lumpectomy and I'll be recommending a course of chemotherapy and radiation, but there's no reason to think she will have anything other than a full recovery. There will be regular check-ups after that to make sure there hasn't been a recurrence, but I'd say the prognosis is very good.''

For the second time that morning, Cassie's tears

flowed unchecked. She clasped the doctor's hand. "Thank you."

"No need. I was just doing my job."

"Can I see her?"

"She's still in recovery. Why not go and have your lunch, then come back. She'll be in her room by then. I'll check in on her later. If all goes as I anticipate, she'll be released in the morning."

Cassie and her friends were exchanging joyful hugs when Cole and Jake arrived.

"Good news?" Cole asked, his gaze on Cassie.

She nodded. "The best. The surgeon expects her to make a full recovery."

Genuine relief washed over his face. "I'm glad."

"Grandma's going to be okay?" Jake asked as if he didn't dare to believe it. "Really?"

Cassie gave him a hug, wanting to believe in that as much as he did. "Absolutely," she said with confidence. If a positive outlook and the support of family and friends had anything to do with it, her mother would not only survive, she would thrive. "She'll have some treatments for a while, but that should do the trick."

"I propose we all go out and celebrate," Cole said. "My treat."

"I never turn down a man with a credit card in his hand," Gina teased. "Especially when the alternative is hospital cafeteria food. Let's do it."

They found a lovely restaurant just a few blocks away from the hospital. Cassie actually managed to eat with enthusiasm for the first time in several days. Not even the sight of Jake sitting side by side with his father could take away the relief she'd felt when the doctor had given his report.

Her mother was going to survive. She had said the words, had tried not to let her faith waver for a single second, but until the surgeon had spoken with such optimism, she hadn't really dared to believe it.

"You okay?" Cole asked, leaning close to whisper in her ear.

"I am now," she said. "Thank you for arranging for her to come here."

"It was the least I could do."

"But you didn't have to do it."

"Yes, I did," he insisted. "For a lot of reasons, not the least of which is that she's your mother."

Cassie refused to let herself read anything at all into that. She was just grateful that everything had turned out as well as it had so far.

"I need to call Stella. If she doesn't object, I'd like to stay tonight, then Jake and I can go back tomorrow with my mother. If you need to get home, I'm sure Lauren will take the three of us back. She chartered a plane."

"I'm staying," Cole said flatly. "I've already made arrangements to keep the suite another night. And if the doctor says your mother should have her chemo and radiation here, when the time comes we'll reserve the suite for as long as necessary."

Cassie hadn't even considered what arrangements might have to be made for the follow-up treatments. "Cole, we can't keep imposing on you like that. I'm sure whatever she needs can be done in Laramie."

"She's going to have the best," he insisted. "We'll let the doctor decide."

Because there was no way she could knowingly accept less than the best for her mother, she reluctantly nodded her agreement. She was already in Cole's debt.

It would be foolish to turn down his offer out of stubborn pride.

"Thank you," she said stiffly.

"Like I said, I owe you."

But for what, she wondered. For betraying her? He claimed he hadn't done that, or hadn't meant to, at any rate. Even though he knew his father had likely had some hand in it, he still didn't know the whole truth, that it was his father and her mother who had done the conniving. Would he be so eager to help her mother if he knew that?

She pushed all of that aside when Karen raised a glass in a toast. "To long, healthy lives for all of us and for those we love," she said.

It was a toast that would come back to haunt them. Three hours later, just as Karen, Lauren, Emma and Gina were about to return to Winding River, a call came that Caleb had collapsed at the ranch. By the time they reached the hospital in Laramie, Karen's husband was dead of a massive heart attack at thirty-eight.

The next few days passed in a blur. Cassie alternated between caring for her mother and sitting with her friend, whose pale complexion and glassy, dazed eyes were frightening to behold. None of them were able to reach Karen, no matter how they tried.

Karen got through Caleb's funeral without shedding a single tear. She politely thanked everyone who attended the services, served food to the mourners who visited the ranch, then went about the ranch chores with sporadic surges of frenzied activity, refusing all offers of help. She'd reacted only once—to the arrival of Grady Blackhawk, a man who'd made no secret of the fact he wanted to buy their ranch. Caleb had hated him.

Karen had almost lost it when she'd seen him. Cole had escorted him away from the house.

"She can't go on like this," Lauren said, watching her worriedly after most of the guests had left.

"She needs to cry, to let it out," Gina added. Gina had always been the one most in touch with her emotions—the quickest to cry but also the fastest to laugh.

"I think she's afraid to start," Cassie said. "I think she's terrified that once the tears come, she won't be able to stop. To be honest, I feel that way myself. How could this happen to Caleb? He was so young. A thirty-eight-year-old isn't supposed to be having a heart attack, much less dying from it. There were so many things they planned to do together. They wanted to start a family. It's not fair."

"I feel as if that boy traded his life for mine," her mother said, her expression gloomy. She had insisted on attending the funeral, then stopping by the ranch to offer her condolences.

"Mama, don't you dare say that," Cassie said. "It doesn't work like that."

"Well, it just breaks my heart to see Karen this way," her mother said. "The burden of running this ranch was heavy enough on the two of them. How she'll keep up alone is beyond me. Of all you girls, she was the one I thought was set for life with a nice, steady man by her side. No offense to you, Emma, or you, Lauren, but Caleb was the kind of man all of you should have been looking for."

"No question about that," Lauren agreed. "I certainly had a knack for picking losers."

"Mick wasn't a loser, but he wasn't exactly the dependable, steady guy that Caleb was," Emma said of her own ex.

"What's that about a steady man?" Cole inquired, coming up behind Cassie. He rested his hands on her shoulders, massaging gently.

Ever since they'd gotten the news about Caleb, Cole had been a rock for Karen and all the rest of them. Leaving Cassie and Jake overnight with her mother in Denver, he had accompanied Karen and the others to the hospital in Laramie, then handled all of the funeral arrangements. He seemed to anticipate what needed to be done and took care of it without waiting to be asked. The only thing Karen had refused was his offer to send over help for the ranch.

She had been adamant about that, insisting that the ranch was her responsibility and that she needed to learn to deal with the work on her own. Nothing anyone said could dissuade her.

"I don't like the way she looks," Cassie said worriedly. "She's exhausted. She can't stay here by herself, and that's that."

"Well, we know she's not going to leave, so I'll just have to move in," Lauren said. "I imagine I can still do a few ranch chores."

They all stared. "You?"

"Why not me?" she asked indignantly. "I grew up on a ranch. It hasn't been that long. I still know one end of a cow from the other."

"But, Lauren," Emma protested, "what about your career?"

Lauren waved off the question. "It'll be there when I get back or it won't. I already have more money than I can ever spend. I'm staying here, and that's that."

Gina and Emma agreed to stay that night, as well, so Cassie left with her mother and Cole for the hundred-mile ride back to Winding River. It was late when they arrived, and her mother went straight to bed, but Cassie lingered on the porch with Cole. Jake was spending the night next door, so they were alone.

"Do you honestly think Karen will be able to manage that ranch on her own?" she asked Cole, settling into the swing.

He sat next to her and set the swing into a slow, easy motion. "Ranching is difficult work under the best of conditions. She's going to need help. I get the impression she doesn't have the money to hire on additional hands, and she flatly refused my offer to send one of my men over, even temporarily."

"Maybe she should consider selling. She always wanted to travel. In high school that's all she ever talked about." Even as she said it, though, she knew Karen would never sell the ranch that Caleb had loved. Even if it drained her financially and physically, she would keep it because it had been his dream. But Karen's misplaced sense of loyalty could wind up killing her.

"She won't sell," Cole said with certainty.

Cassie sighed and met his gaze. "I know, but it might be better if she did."

He tucked a curl behind her ear. "We don't always do what's best, even if it's plain as day to us what that is."

Something in his voice told her he was no longer talking about Karen. "What would you do differently if you could?"

"Fight for you," he said without hesitation.

Cassie's breath caught in her throat at the regret she heard in his voice. "Would you?"

His gaze locked with hers. "I should have done it back then. I knew it the second I left town, but by then it was too late. Then I got that note and, well, all I could do was hate you for what I thought was an even worse betrayal than my own.''

Cassie debated telling him what she had learned from his father. Part of her was reluctant to stir up the ashes of the past, but he deserved to know the truth, especially after all he had done for Edna Collins in recent days. ''My mother wrote that note,'' she said flatly, praying that it wouldn't change his commitment to helping with her medical expenses.

Shock washed over his face. ''How do you know that?'' he demanded.

''Your father told me. He admitted that they conspired to keep us apart.''

Cole stood and began to pace. Suddenly he stopped and slammed his fist against a post. ''Dammit! I should have guessed.''

''How could you have guessed? I certainly never imagined it.''

''I saw them with their heads together back then,'' he explained. ''But your mom and I had always gotten along so well, I couldn't believe that she would be involved in splitting us up. I only saw my father's less-than-subtle touch all over it.''

''Well, unless your father lied, which I seriously doubt, she was involved,'' Cassie said flatly. ''I haven't spoken to her about it, but I will, once things settle down and she has her health back.''

Her voice caught at the end, and she put her hands over her face as the tears, never far from the surface, flowed again. Cole sat back down and reached for her.

''It's okay,'' he murmured. ''Don't cry. She's going to be fine.''

''I know, but...'' She looked at him, feeling an overwhelming sense of sorrow. "But Caleb won't be. Karen's lost him forever. How can I be so glad about my mother, when my best friend's husband is dead?"

"One has absolutely nothing to do with the other. Karen understands that. She's as happy as you are that your mother's prognosis is good. She would never begrudge you that. And she knows that you care about her and her loss. She's going to need all of you more than ever. It's good that you've come home. Even better that you and Lauren, at least, intend to stick around."

She dared to meet his gaze then and saw something else in his eyes, something she hadn't dared to hope for in years and years. There was tenderness and longing and hope.

"*I'm* glad you're back to stay," he said softly.

They were words she had longed to hear. His eyes promised things that she had yearned for. And yet she couldn't allow herself to be swept off her feet, caught up in a dream of what might be, now that she was back in Winding River. Not with Jake and the secret of his paternity standing between them.

Because if Cole knew the truth, that she had kept his son from him all these years, whatever fantasy he was spinning about their future would crash and burn under the weight of his justifiable fury. He might eventually forgive his father's actions, but he would never forgive her for keeping such a secret. Never. And if he was inclined to, Frank Davis would have quite a lot to say about having the Davis heir kept from them.

"I have to go in," she said, pulling away, putting a safe distance between them.

"Why? It's not that late."

"But I have to be at Stella's for the morning shift tomorrow," she said.

"Come on," he chided. "Surely you don't need that much beauty sleep."

"You'd be surprised."

"Then have dinner with me tomorrow night, you and Jake."

"No," she said, more harshly than she should have.

He regarded her quizzically. "Why not?"

"Because I need to go to the ranch to see Karen," she said at once, praying that he would accept the excuse.

"Then I'll drive you."

If she refused him, he would want to know why, and she didn't have a single answer that he would accept without dissecting it.

"Fine," she said with undisguised reluctance.

"Thank you, Cole," he mocked.

She sighed. "I'm sorry. I do appreciate it, really I do. You've been a rock through all of this. I know Karen is grateful, too."

He regarded her doubtfully, but let it go. "Then I'll see you about three. Does that give you enough time after your shift ends?"

"Three will be fine."

"Maybe I'll stop by earlier and spend some time with Jake."

Cassie's heart skidded to a stop. "I...I don't think that's a good idea," she said, scrambling to come up with a reason he would buy. None came to mind.

Cole studied her quietly for what seemed to be an eternity, then asked, "Is there a reason you don't want me around Jake? This isn't the first time I've sensed that you'd just as soon I steer clear of him."

"I just don't want him to start to count on you. It's hard on a boy if men come and go in his life."

His gaze narrowed. "Have a lot of men come and gone in Jake's life?"

"No, because I have been very careful not to let that happen."

"I won't let him down," Cole said.

"You say that, but you can't guarantee it."

"Any more than you can," he replied. "We're all human. We all disappoint the people we care about from time to time, even with the best intentions. But I swear to you, Cassie, I would never knowingly hurt him."

"You wouldn't mean to," she agreed. "But it's inevitable."

"You would rather deprive him of my company than risk having me hurt him?"

"Yes," she said flatly. "That's how it has to be."

"For a woman who once thrived on risks, you've grown up to be a cautious woman."

"I was burned," she said simply. "I learned my lesson."

He studied her with a disconcerting intensity, then asked, "Who did that to you, Cassie?"

She regarded him incredulously. "You have to ask?"

"It wasn't just me. It couldn't have been. Was it Jake's father? Did he disappoint you badly, too?"

"Yes," she said, seizing the explanation. He had no idea how true it was. "Jake's father made it impossible for me ever to trust another man."

Cole leveled a look into her eyes that burned right through to her soul. "I'm going to change that," he vowed. "Just wait and see."

But he couldn't, she thought as he dropped a tender kiss on her forehead and walked away. Of all the men in the world, Cole Davis was the one least likely to be able to change the way she felt about trust.

And if he knew the truth about Jake, he'd feel the exact same way about her.

Chapter Ten

Cole took Cassie's reluctance to let him get too involved in her son's life as a challenge. Not only did he intend to convince her she was wrong about that, he intended to win her heart again.

Of course, trying to court a woman whose mother was ill and whose best friend was in mourning required a bit of inventiveness. Overt attempts to sweep her off her feet would, no doubt, be met with dismay. That left subtlety, something the Davis men were not known for. He'd inherited his father's inclination to go after what he wanted, no holds barred. Restraining that impulse was going to be tricky, but he could do it. He had to. The stakes were too high to risk losing.

As promised, he arrived at Cassie's promptly at three to drive her to Karen's. He came with a new computer game for Jake, flowers for Mrs. Collins and nothing at all for Cassie. A faint flicker of disappointment in her eyes was his reward. Next time he knew she wouldn't be so quick to turn down whatever token offering he brought for her.

Meantime, Jake was staring at the computer game with a mix of excitement and unmistakable frustration that Cole couldn't quite interpret.

"Anything wrong, pal? I thought you'd like that game. It's just hit the market. You don't have it, do you?"

Jake shook his head. "It's great, but..." He shot a condemning look at his mother, then muttered, "I don't have a computer. Mom won't get me one, especially after what happened where we used to live."

"Jake Collins, don't you dare imply that I refused to buy you a computer out of spite or something," Cassie said. "You know perfectly well it's not some sort of punishment. We simply can't afford one, though I have to admit you didn't display any evidence that you can use one responsibly."

Cole was about to speak, but one look at her face kept him silent. If he made an offer to buy the computer, it was evident she wouldn't appreciate it. Besides, he understood why she might be reluctant for the boy to have a computer after the trouble he'd gotten into on the Internet.

"Maybe we can think about getting a computer for Christmas," Mrs. Collins said.

"But that's months and months away," Jake protested. "This game is so cool. I want to play it now."

Cole locked gazes with Cassie. "How about if I loan you an old computer I have at the house for now? We can leave off the modem so there will be no Internet hookup."

"I don't know," she said, clearly hesitant.

"Mom, please," Jake pleaded.

"It's just a loan," Cole insisted. "And it's just gathering dust out at the ranch."

She sighed. "Okay, if you're sure you have it to spare. And definitely no modem."

Little did she know that he had half a dozen tucked away, thanks to the rapidly changing technology and his own need to be on the cutting edge of the industry. He could have supplied her with one that was state of the art without batting an eye, but he resolved to provide an older model that wouldn't get her dander up.

"No Internet," Cassie said pointedly. "Understood?"

Jake sighed heavily. "Okay."

Cole gave the boy's shoulder a squeeze. "I'll bring it by tomorrow, Jake. How will that be?"

"All right," the boy said eagerly. "And you'll show me how to write a program?"

"Sure, if you want to learn," he said, then cautioned, "It's a lot of work."

"That's okay. Someday I'm going to start my own computer technology company just like you." He grabbed Cole's hand. "Come look at my room and we can decide where the computer should go when you bring it."

Cole found Jake's budding case of hero worship touching. After living for the past few years with his own computer-illiterate father, a man who had absolutely no appreciation for his work, it was nice to have someone so eager to understand it and share in it. Jake was a good kid. Cassie had done a terrific job raising him on her own. Cole reminded himself to tell her that.

But when he tried to bring up the subject on the ride to Karen's ranch, Cassie's response was as touchy as always when he mentioned Jake. Cole told himself that her reaction was simply that of an overly protective single mom, but he was having difficulty believing it. Calling her on it would accomplish nothing. He'd already tried that, and she had only become more defensive.

Maybe he would ask Mrs. Collins. Her attitude toward him seemed to be mellowing lately. Maybe she would give him a straight answer. If not, he would just have to count on the fact that one of these days, Cassie would trust him enough to be completely honest with him. By nature, she wasn't a secretive person.

At least she hadn't been ten years ago, he reminded himself. Ten years was a long time, especially when most of that time she had been raising a child on her own. The truth was, he had no idea how Cassie might have changed. He just knew that plenty of things about her were the same, enough to fascinate him all over again.

He glanced at her, distressed to see that she was staring out the window with a distant, sad expression on her face. Maybe she was merely thinking about her friend's loss, but he doubted it. He had caught that same expression even before Caleb's death. Something—or someone—had stolen her youthful vibrancy and optimism, and Cole wouldn't rest until he knew how that had happened.

Over the next few weeks Cassie lived in terror that Cole was going to learn the truth. It had become evident that he suspected that she was keeping something from him. And he also seemed to sense that it had to do with Jake. When he'd first tried to pin her down about her reasons for wanting to keep them apart, pure panic had washed through her. She'd had to force herself to calm down and respond as if her behavior was merely the reaction of a single mom.

She had thought at the time that Cole had bought her explanation about not allowing Jake to start counting on anyone who wasn't likely to be around permanently. She'd also tried to be less overt about keeping the two of them apart, finding legitimate excuses to get Jake out of the house whenever Cole was likely to stop by. She'd been pleased by her success.

But then Cole had brought over that blasted computer, and it was clear that he intended to stick around and teach Jake to use it. When she'd tried to protest, the look he'd given her told her that nothing she said was going to be convincing. He was on to her, and sooner or later he was going to demand answers.

If her own determination to keep silent were the only thing at issue, she was sure the secret of Jake's paternity would be safe enough, but there was Frank Davis to consider. She didn't trust Cole's father not to tell him everything. It had been evident during their confrontation that he wanted, in fact expected, Cole to claim Jake as the Davis heir. She doubted he would patiently wait forever for that to happen.

As it had ever since her return home, the debate over what to do raged in her head, setting off yet another dull, throbbing headache.

"Cassie, are you okay?" her mother asked weakly.

She forced a smile and turned back to the bed where her mother was resting after her first radiation treatment. The trip to Denver was more tiring for her than the treatment itself.

"I'm fine," Cassie fibbed.

"You're worried about the amount of time Jake and Cole are spending together, aren't you?"

"I've done everything I can to keep them apart," she admitted. "I don't know what else to do, short of telling Cole the truth."

"Why not do that?" she said. "Face it, Cassie. He's going to figure it out sooner or later. Wouldn't it be better if the truth came from you?"

Cassie knew her mother was right, but she simply hadn't been able to work up the courage to say the words. "I don't know how to tell him, not after all this time."

"Would you like me to do it?"

She shook her head. "No, I have to be the one." She faced her mother, grateful for this opening. "There's something I don't understand."

"What?"

"Why are you and Frank Davis both so eager for the truth to come out, when years ago you couldn't wait to break us up?"

What little color there had been in her mother's cheeks faded. "Why..." she began, but her voice faltered. "Why would you say something like that?"

"I know, Mom. Mr. Davis told me all about the letter you kept from me, the one in which Cole explained why he had to leave. He also told me about the letter you wrote to Cole telling him I didn't want him in my life anymore."

Tears tracked down her mother's cheeks. She reached for Cassie's hand. Her frail grasp was icy cold. "I'm sorry. We thought it was for the best."

"You mean Mr. Davis thought it was best."

"No," her mother said sharply. "We agreed. You were both too young."

"But I was having a baby, and you've already admitted that you knew it was Cole's. Things might have been so different."

"No," her mother said just as adamantly. "Nothing would have been any different. Frank would never have approved of a marriage between the two of you. He would have found a way to stop it. Once I knew about the baby, I told him—in fact, I begged him—to let you and Cole work it out, but he refused. I would have gone to Cole myself, but I didn't know where he was. Frank gave me the money for your medical expenses. He promised me more if I let things be, but I never took another dime."

She squeezed Cassie's hand. "Not another dime," she repeated.

"Oh, Mom," Cassie whispered wearily. "You should have gone ahead and taken the money. The damage was done."

"I couldn't. I already felt guilty enough. I could barely look you in the face. When Jake was born, I thought of all we could have done for him with that money, but by then it was too late. And that wasn't the worst of it. When Cole came by here to visit, to ask after you, I slammed the door on him. I couldn't bear to face him after what I'd done to keep you apart, to keep him from his own son."

Her mother sighed. "I shudder to think what would have happened to me if he knew all of that. He certainly wouldn't have offered to pay my medical expenses."

"Yes he would," Cassie reassured her. "And he does know, because I told him that much at least. I told him about the letters."

"When?"

"A few weeks ago, right after your surgery."

"And he never said a word," her mother said, looking amazed. "And all this time he's been paying for my radiation treatments and taking me to Denver."

Cassie nodded.

"That should tell you something, then."

"What?"

"If he can forgive me, then surely he'll be able to forgive you."

Cassie wanted desperately to believe that, but what she had done wasn't the same. It wasn't the same thing at all. She had once professed to love Cole, and yet she had kept their child a secret from him...and was continuing to do so.

Despite all of Cassie's warnings and her threats of dire punishments, she knew that Jake was still trying to come up with ways to sneak off to the Davis ranch. Maybe it was simply the lure of the forbidden. More likely it was hero worship.

So far she'd caught Jake half a dozen times on the outskirts of town, riding the bike he'd repaired. At this rate the boy was going to be grounded until he hit thirty. It didn't seem to faze him, though. He simply tried a more inventive approach the next time.

As if that weren't nerve-racking enough, since Jake wasn't going to him, Cole continued to stop by her house unannounced, bringing thoughtful treats for her mother and disconcerting kisses for her. She hadn't figured out a way to get the man to keep his hands and his mouth to himself. He had history on his side. She hadn't been able to do it ten years ago, either.

She had just kicked off her shoes and propped her feet on the porch railing, when Cole's car turned into the driveway. He emerged in a pair of faded jeans that hugged his hips, and a T-shirt that stretched taut over his broad shoulders. It was hard to imagine that this was the same man whose computer company had just reported earnings in the millions. She sighed when she thought about it. If they had been a lousy match ten years ago, there was an even greater divide between them now. He was a college-educated business whiz. She was a waitress with a high school diploma.

"Why are you here?" she inquired testily.

Undaunted by her attitude, he shot her a grin. "To improve your mood, for starters."

"Exactly how are you planning to do that?" she inquired warily.

"I'm going to take you away from all this. Get your bathing suit."

"Why?"

"This is an impulsive moment, darlin'. Stop asking so many questions. I never used to have to work so hard to persuade you to come with me. I seem to recall a time when you couldn't wait to sneak off to be alone with me."

"I'm older and wiser now."

"More's the pity." He nudged her bare, aching feet off the railing. "Get a move on."

"Maybe I don't enjoy swimming," she said grumpily.

"Since when?"

"Since right this second."

He sighed heavily and sat beside her. "Okay, spill it. What's really going on here? Did somebody sneak out of Stella's today without paying the bill? Did somebody stiff you on your tip?"

"Everything at work went just fine."

"Then this grouchiness has to do with me?"

Him, the situation, the lies, everything. Her life was a mess. Not that she admitted any of that. Unfortunately, he seemed to interpret her silence as agreement.

"What did I do?" he asked.

"Nothing," she admitted. "You've been great."

"But?"

Finally she leveled a look straight at him and repeated her earlier question. "Why are you here?"

"To take you swimming."

"But why?"

"Because it's a hot day and I thought we could cool off in the river, then have a picnic. That used to be your favorite way to spend a summer evening."

It had also been what had gotten them into trouble. Being alone and scantily clad had led to steamy kisses and eventually, on that one memorable night, to making love. He wasn't fooling her one bit. That was exactly the way he saw the evening ending tonight, too.

"I'm not as young and foolish as I once was."

He frowned at that. "What is that supposed to mean?"

"I am not interested in letting you seduce me."

She had expected anger or at the very least irritation, but instead he chuckled.

"Okay, then, *you* can seduce *me*," he said cheerfully. "I'm easy."

"No seduction, period."

He shrugged, as if it didn't matter a bit to him one way or the other. "Suit yourself. Bring Jake along as a chaperon."

As if he'd been lurking just inside the door waiting for a chance to join them, Jake stepped onto the porch and let the screen door slam shut behind him.

"Bring me where? And what's a chaperon?"

"You are grounded, young man," Cassie said, regarding him sternly. "You're not going anywhere. And eavesdropping is not polite."

"But, Mom…"

"Inside," she said, gesturing in that direction. "You know the rules."

"You're ruining my whole summer," he protested. He inched closer to Cole. "Tell her."

Though Cole looked as if he wanted to ask a whole lot of questions, he merely shrugged. "She's your mother. You do as she says."

"But it's not fair. What did I do that was so wrong? I just wanted to go over to see Cole. He said I could." He gazed up at Cole. "Didn't you? You said I could come anytime."

"With your mother's permission," Cole reminded him. "Is that what this is all about? You were sneaking off to the ranch again?"

"More than once," Cassie told him before facing Jake. "Inside now, or I swear I'll add another day to your grounding."

Tears welled up in Jake's eyes. "I hate you!" he shouted. "I hate you and I wish we'd never come here!"

The words cut through her like well-aimed knives, but she couldn't relent. She simply couldn't. What she was doing was for the best.

But then Jake whirled away from her, and instead of going inside as she'd ordered, he threw himself at Cole. "I wish you were my dad. Then I could come and live with you."

Dismay welled up in her throat. She wanted to cry out, to protest. She didn't think she'd reacted aloud, but she must have, because Cole's gaze shot to hers and suddenly she saw that he knew, that in that instant he'd guessed the truth she had been trying so desperately to hide.

She also saw the cold rage in his eyes as it stripped away the warmth she'd come to yearn for.

"Son," he said, his voice faltering ever so slightly. His hand rested for just an instant on Jake's head. Finally he added, "Do as your mother asked, Jake. Go inside."

Jake seemed to sense that the mood on the porch had shifted in some way. Though his expression remained sullen, he went into the house, but not without slamming the door emphatically behind him.

Cassie waited, frozen, for Cole to say something, anything.

His gaze was damning.

"Is it true?" he asked eventually. "Is Jake my son?"

She tried to speak, tried desperately to find the right words, but none came. Finally she just nodded.

"And all this time you never said a word," he said, regarding her with disbelief. "Not one single word."

"You'd left me," she reminded him. "What was I supposed to do, run after you?"

He winced at that, but his expression didn't soften. "Yes," he said. "You were supposed to come after me. I had a right to know."

"You left me," she repeated. "You had no rights. None at all."

"That boy in there is my son," he all but shouted. At her frantic glance toward the house, he lowered his voice. "I had rights, dammit! And so did he. He had the right not to be born a bastard. He had the right to have my name, my love.''

''It wouldn't have happened that way,'' Cassie said flatly, knowing that his father would have prevented it. Her mother had been right about that. Frank Davis had admitted as much himself. His attitude now might have changed, but back then he would never have permitted a marriage between his son and a girl with no education and no well-connected family. Even now he wanted Cole to claim Jake, not her.

''Well, we'll never know that now, will we?'' Cole said bitterly. He regarded her as if he'd never seen her before. ''I thought I knew you.''

''You knew the woman I used to be, the girl. I've changed, Cole.''

''Obviously,'' he said derisively.

''Because I've had to. While you've been off making your millions, I've been struggling to make ends meet. Instead of going off to college, I had a baby. Instead of being right here in Winding River with family and old friends, I've been living with strangers. I've been doing the best I could to see that my son was loved and fed and educated.''

''*Our* son, dammit. *Ours!*''

Something beyond the words, something in his tone, terrified her. It had gotten proprietary.

''Jake is mine,'' she repeated fiercely. ''In every way that counts, he is mine. Biologically, you might be his father, but you've never done anything for him, never stayed up when he was sick, never read him a story, never comforted him during a storm.''

Cole's eyes blazed with fury. ''And whose fault is that? Don't start throwing that in my face, Cassie,'' he warned. ''It won't hold up. If I've failed as a father, it's because I was never given the chance to be one, and the blame for that lies with you, no one else. Just you."

She was going about this all wrong. Every word out of her mouth was making him angrier, reminding him that she had cost him nine years with his son.

"Maybe…maybe you should leave now," she suggested tentatively. "Go home and think about this. You'll see that I had no choice."

At least she prayed that he would.

But Cole wasn't finished with her yet. "You know," he said, "even if I were to accept that back then you were young and scared, that you thought I'd abandoned you, it wouldn't explain the past few weeks. We'd cleared up the old misunderstandings. We both knew the truth about how we were manipulated by our parents. We were starting to build a future together—at least that's what I was hoping for. And still you kept silent."

"I was afraid," she admitted.

"Of what?"

She didn't dare voice it. She couldn't tell him that she was terrified that he would do as his father expected, that he would want to claim his son, that he would try to take Jake away from her. Saying the words might plant the idea in his head.

"I just was," she said, leaving it at that.

Cole regarded her with disgust. "The old Cassie would never have given in to fear. The old Cassie would have trusted me with the truth."

"But don't you see?" she said softly. "The old Cassie doesn't exist anymore."

Cole sighed heavily. "And it's plain that I don't know the new one at all."

Chapter Eleven

How could he have been so blind?

Cole asked himself that a hundred times on the drive back to his ranch. Now that he knew the truth, he could see that the boy was the spitting image of him, not just in looks, but in interests and attitude.

The photo albums at the Double D were probably stuffed with pictures of him at Jake's age, all taken shortly before his mother's death. He'd bet that any one of those would have shown the unmistakable resemblance. Of course, all those albums were gathering dust in the attic and had been for years. His father wasn't an especially sentimental man.

Still, Cole should have seen it. It had been so clear in that split second between the time Jake had uttered his wistful cry about wishing Cole were his father and Cassie's own cry of dismay. He hadn't needed to look into her eyes to know the truth, but he had, and it was there, plain as day.

And if he were being honest, he had also seen the genuine fear, and a part of him understood it, even sympathized with it. He didn't want to, but he did. Davis men took what they wanted. His father's reputation for ruthlessness was widely known. Cassie had no reason to believe that he was any different. Though she hadn't said it, it was evident that she was terrified that he was going to take her son away from her.

"What are you going to do?" she'd asked just as he'd walked off. There had been no mistaking the fear, the vulnerability, behind the question, or the slight hitch in her voice.

He'd turned and faced her, his thoughts in turmoil, his heart aching. "I don't know," he'd told her honestly.

Until tonight he had truly believed they were getting past all the old hurts and betrayals and building something solid this time, something that could last. It was what he had desperately come to want over the past few weeks. Years ago they had loved with the reckless passion of youth. Since Cassie's return, he'd started to anticipate a future built on the more mature love of two adults who knew their own minds and hearts, two people who would no longer let anything or anyone stand in their way.

Now he'd discovered his fantasy had been spun from a web of lies and omissions. It was the latter that were the most painful to bear. For weeks now his own son had been right under his nose and he hadn't known, hadn't had a clue. Shouldn't he have had at least an inkling, a tiny suspicion? He blamed himself for that, but he blamed Cassie for more—for nine long years he'd lost forever.

He thought of all the suspicions he'd had, the evidence that Cassie had been trying her level best to keep him and Jake apart. Now he knew why, but it was the one reason that had never once crossed his mind, because a deception of such magnitude had seemed impossible. Cassie had always been the one person who was unfailingly straight with him, the one person he could count on to say exactly what she meant. His father? That was another story, but Cassie had always spoken from the heart. That was why he had taken that letter at face value years ago.

When he walked into his house after the long drive home from Cassie's, all he wanted was a stiff drink and some time to himself, time to wrestle with this new turn of events.

Instead, his father greeted him. "You look like something the cat dragged in. You and Cassie have a spat?" he asked, zeroing in on the problem with unerring accuracy.

"Something like that," Cole said wryly. It was definitely a massive understatement.

His father's gaze turned sharp. He studied Cole's face, then gave a little nod of satisfaction. "She finally told you, then?"

As understanding dawned, Cole stared at him. "You know? You know that Jake is my son?"

"Well, of course I know," he boasted, clearly oblivious to Cole's barely concealed surge of anger.

"How long?" Cole asked, his voice deadly calm as he grappled with this newest revelation.

"I suspected it years ago, after you'd left to go back to school, but I didn't have any proof. Not at first, anyway. Then, finally, I got Edna Collins to admit it. Took a whole lot of persuading, I'll tell you that. The woman would have taken the information to her grave, if I hadn't dangled some cash in front of her.''

Leave it to his father to buy what he wanted. "When was that?" Cole asked.

"A month or so after Cassie left town. I guessed she was pregnant. Why else would the girl turn her back on her only family?"

"But you saw no reason to share that with me?"

"No," he said, regarding Cole evenly. "For a time I let myself believe it was better to leave things the way they were. You would have wanted to do the right thing, no matter what kind of mess it made of your life. So I took care of the girl's medical expenses. I offered more, the same as you would have done, but Edna turned me down flat."

"You offered more," Cole repeated derisively. "Money, I imagine."

"Well, of course. What else?"

"You didn't consider offering marriage, maybe righting the wrong I had done by getting Cassie pregnant in the first place?"

His father scowled. "I told you, I wasn't going to let you mess up your life."

"I don't see how taking responsibility for my own actions would have messed up my life. It might have taught me a lesson. And of course there was the fact that I loved the boy's mother."

"That girl was no good for you, that much was plain as day. She was a nobody." At Cole's muttered expletive, he backed down. "At least, that's how I viewed it then."

Cole regarded him curiously, wondering about the

kind of logic his father used to justify his actions. "And now?"

"I've been forced to reevaluate," he conceded.

Which explained the attempts to push him and Cassie together. "And why is that?"

"You weren't showing any signs of getting over the woman. You haven't had a single serious relationship in all the years you've been back. When I heard Cassie was coming back, I decided enough was enough. I couldn't sit by and let the Davis heir be raised as a bastard right under our noses."

Suddenly all of the evening's stress boiled over. Infuriated, Cole grabbed a fistful of his father's shirt and dragged him close until they were practically nose to nose. "How dare you?"

"I did what I had to do."

"Then this is all about your choices, your decisions?" It took every bit of restraint he possessed to keep from shaking his father. "That boy was mine—hell, he was *your* grandson—and you kept it to yourself. What were you thinking?"

Not bothering to wait for an answer, he released his father and backed off before he could take the swing at him he so desperately wanted to take. "You're the same manipulative, controlling son of a bitch I left home to escape ten years ago."

His father drew himself up, seemingly unfazed by Cole's anger. "I'm your father, and I'll thank you to show a little respect," he commanded.

"Then you'll have to work damn hard to prove you deserve it. Right now I don't see it," Cole snapped, then whirled and headed up the stairs.

In his room he dragged out a suitcase and began haphazardly filling it with clothes. He had no idea where he was going, but he knew he had to get away. He heard his father huffing and puffing as he climbed the stairs, but he ignored it.

"Dammit, boy, where do you think you're going?" his father demanded, hanging on to the doorjamb as he caught his breath.

"Away from here."

"You've just found out you have a son and you're leaving?" the old man asked incredulously.

"I have to think, and I sure as hell can't do it here under your roof."

"I'd like to know why not? The Double D is your home. It's your heritage."

"Not because I want it," Cole pointed out. "Because you insist on it. If I stay, I'll never know if what I decide is right or what you've deliberately set out to plant in my head."

"That boy belongs here with us. It couldn't be any clearer," his father said.

"To you, maybe." Then the full significance of what his father had said sank in. "*Jake* belongs here? Not Cassie? Is that what you're saying? Even now, knowing that she's the mother of my child, you still don't think she's good enough?"

"Hasn't she proved that by lying to you?"

Cole couldn't argue the point, not successfully, when he was still spitting mad over that himself. He let it go and continued packing.

"Cole, don't do this," his father pleaded. "Don't give Cassie time to get herself an attorney, maybe even to take off again. Stay here and claim what's yours."

Cole silently closed the suitcase, then turned to face his father. "Jake is mine, not yours. The decision is mine, too. I want you to steer clear of him and stay the hell out of it. You've already done more than enough.''

His father shook his head. ''You're making a mistake.''

''It's mine to make.''

That said, he left the room and the house. He had to wonder, as he drove away from the Double D, if he would ever be able to come back, knowing the part his father had played in everything that had happened.

Cassie sat on the front porch, trembling and sick at heart, long after Cole had left. When Jake crept outside to sit beside her, she wrapped him in a hug and clung to him until he protested.

''Mom, why did you and Cole fight?'' he asked when she reluctantly released him. ''I could hear you.''

Her blood ran cold. ''How much did you hear?''

''Not the words, just that he sounded real mad. Was he mad?''

''Very,'' she admitted.

''How come?''

''I...I kept something from him that I shouldn't have.''

Did she dare tell Jake the rest? Not yet, she concluded, not until she and Cole had worked things out, if that was even possible. She needed to know what he wanted, how much a part of Jake's life he intended to be, how much of a fight she might have on her hands.

''I like him, Mom. He's been teaching me stuff, and he doesn't talk down to me like I'm a dumb kid.''

''I know. He thinks you're pretty special. He's said so.''

Jake regarded her worriedly. ''I didn't mean what I said before about hating you.''

She managed a faint smile. "I know that."

"You're the best. And I like being here with Grandma, too. I don't want to leave Winding River. We aren't going to, are we?"

No, Cassie thought, for better or worse, they were here to stay. She wasn't going to run again. Why bother, when Cole had the resources to find her wherever she went, anyway? And he would hunt her down. She had no doubts about that.

The next day, though, she was stunned to discover that Cole had left town.

"Went out to Silicon Valley," one of Frank's friends reported when he showed up for breakfast at Stella's. He regarded her speculatively. "I don't suppose *you* know anything about that?"

"Not a thing," she said honestly, not certain whether to be relieved by the news or not.

Adding to the puzzle was the fact that Frank himself was a no-show at Stella's. He hadn't missed a day there in forty years or more.

"Frank took it real hard," Pete reported as Cassie poured his coffee. "Despite all his grumbling, he dotes on that boy. I stopped by the ranch on my way here, but he wouldn't even get out of bed. Said if Cole was gone for good, he didn't have any reason to live."

"That's nonsense," Cassie said.

"That's what I told him, but you know Frank. He's always been the dramatic type. Likes to control things, too. He'll moan and groan for a few days, then come out swinging like always."

No one knew that better than Cassie. "Yes, I'm sure he'll pull himself together," she agreed. "I'll get your eggs now, Pete."

"Don't forget the bacon and hash browns."

She grinned at him. "As if I could. You've been having the exact same breakfast for the past twelve years."

"More than that," he said, grinning back at her. "Started before your time. Of course, I have to have it here at Stella's. If my wife found out, she'd have my hide."

"I imagine she guessed your little secret years ago."

Pete sighed. "Probably so. Never could keep a thing from that woman. That's the basis of a good marriage, you know, keeping everything out in the open. Remember that when your wedding day comes along, and you won't go wrong."

Unfortunately, it was too late for that advice to do Cassie any good at all.

The discovery that his father knew the truth and had chosen to hide it had been the final bitter blow on the worst night of Cole's entire life. After driving aimlessly for most of the night, he took off for Silicon Valley and a round of business meetings he'd been postponing for months. He left word on his father's answering machine that that's where he'd be until further notice.

He'd expected the change of scenery to give him some perspective. He'd also hoped that the steady lineup of strategy meetings and technology discussions would keep him focused on work. He didn't want to think about Jake or Cassie or his father. The wound was still too raw.

Unfortunately, he'd never been much good at avoiding tough decisions. Facing things squarely and dealing with them was the way he conducted business.

He managed to prolong his stay in California for a month, but Cassie was never far from his thoughts.

Was his father right? Would she bolt with Jake now that the truth was out? She was certainly terrified enough to try. His only consolation was that the world wasn't big enough to swallow her up so completely that he couldn't find her again. Few people vanished without a trace, and Cassie wasn't clever enough or rich enough to be one of them.

Of course, she had been clever enough to keep his son away from him for nine long years. He'd missed Jake's birth, his first step, his first word. Things that he could never get back. The lack of memories weighed on him. Eventually the prospect of missing so much as a minute more of his son's life had him reaching for the phone, something he should have done days or even weeks earlier.

When Cassie picked up on the first ring, he breathed a sigh of relief. "You're there," he said.

"Where else would I be?"

She sounded resigned.

"I wasn't sure you'd stick around."

"Running would have been pointless," she said, all but admitting she'd considered it. "Besides, my mother and Karen need me here."

"And that's the only reason you stayed?"

She remained silent so long he thought she might not answer.

"No," she said at last. "We have to deal with this for Jake's sake."

"I'm glad you realize that."

"I've always had my son's best interests at heart."

Cole barely bit back a sharp retort. "Now's not the time to debate that," he said. "I'll be home in a few days. We'll talk then."

He hung up without waiting for her reply. He'd discovered two things by making that call—one reassuring, one disconcerting. He now knew that Cassie would be waiting when he returned to Winding River. And, God help him, he also knew just how much that mattered to him.

When Cole drove into Winding River a few days later, his mind was made up at last. He'd lost the first nine years of his son's life. He didn't intend to lose the next nine or any thereafter. This wasn't about revenge or even justice. It was about a father forming a bond with his son, a bond he'd been denied up until now.

He arrived on Cassie's doorstep prepared to start the custody fight to end all custody fights.

She greeted him with pale cheeks and frightened eyes, then stepped onto the porch and closed the door securely behind her. He couldn't help noticing that she had lost weight she could hardly spare in the month he'd been gone. Even so, she was the most beautiful woman he'd ever known, and his heart lurched into the familiar rhythm of desire.

"What are you going to do?" she asked straight-out, not even trying to mask her fear.

One look into her eyes and his determination faltered. He knew he couldn't do what he'd planned. He couldn't take her son—their son—away from her. Whatever else he thought of her, she'd been a good mother and Jake loved her. Separating them would be a hollow victory.

Besides, there was no denying that even after all that had happened, he wanted her. Bitterness wasn't quite enough to bury lust. The heat of anger felt awfully damn close to the heat of passion.

"Marry me," he said before he could stop himself.

Clearly taken by surprise, she blinked hard, then shook her head. "No, not if this is just some way for you to claim your son."

"You don't have a choice," he said mildly.

"Of course I do."

"If you don't marry me, I'll fight you for Jake—and I guarantee you, I'll win. There are some perks to being a Davis in this state, and that's one of them."

"You would use your father's power?" she asked in a whisper, then shook her head. "What was I thinking? Of course you would. And I imagine you have a fair share of power yourself these days. Everyone warned me, but I wanted to believe you were better than that."

"Once upon a time I thought so, too," he said wearily. "Not anymore. Just remember, darlin', you started this when you kept Jake from me. I'm just playing by the winner-take-all rules you set."

"But marriage?" she said. "It would be a mockery. Surely there has to be another way. We could make an arrangement of some kind."

"So that I can spend a few hours each week with my son?" He shook his head. "Not nearly good enough. Marriage is my best offer. Take it or leave it. Otherwise I sue for custody."

She stared at him with such a look of despair that he almost wavered, but not quite. He knew he was bullying her, but at the moment he didn't really give a damn. He told himself that she would like the alternative even less.

"I need some time," she whispered finally.

"Time for what? To think it over? To run?"

Her chin came up at that. "I've already told you, I'm not running."

"Good. I'm glad you see the futility in that. Okay," he said, relenting, "you can have a few days to think it over. Go to Emma if you want to and ask her legal opinion about whether I can force you to do this."

When she winced, he knew he had been dead on about her intention.

"She'll only tell you that my case for custody is very strong, whether I use my influence in this state or not."

"You've already consulted an attorney, then," she said, her voice flat.

"Did you honestly think I wouldn't?"

"I was hoping we could work this out between the two of us without getting a bunch of lawyers involved."

"We can," he said. "All you have to do is marry me. Then you and I will raise Jake together. We'll be a family."

"Will we?" she asked, regarding him with skepticism. "Exactly what kind of family can we have if the only reason we're together is your determination to be a real father to Jake?"

"I don't know," he said honestly. "I don't have a whole lot of experience with picture-book family life. I grew up with a manipulative father who has done his utmost to control me. I fell in love with a woman who kept my own son a secret. Obviously, I've missed a few lessons on what it takes to make a family."

He leveled a look straight into her eyes. "By the same token, I can tell you a whole lot about lies and deceit."

She weathered the attack without flinching. "Cole, this will be a disaster," she said, a pleading note in her voice. "Can't you see that?"

"Then we'll just be living up to those low expectations everyone had for us years ago," he said without emotion. "Seems to me like a fitting end to our so-called love story, don't you think?"

Her complexion went even paler at his mocking remark, but to her credit she didn't shed a single tear.

"I'll give you my answer on Sunday," she said at last. And then, as if to get in a mocking blow of her own, she added, "Right after church."

Unfortunately, Cole was relatively certain that no matter how many prayers were uttered, there were no heavenly answers for the two of them. Their sorry fate had been decided a long time ago by people right here on earth.

Chapter Twelve

Cassie felt sick to her stomach. Marrying Cole—once her most powerful fantasy—was now nothing more than a way to keep her son. How could she go through with such a travesty? How could Cole?

But, judging from his cold, distant demeanor, he had no intention of backing down. He saw this as a generous gesture…and maybe, under the circumstances, it was. She couldn't help thinking, though, that it was little better than blackmail.

Maybe she didn't deserve any better after what she'd done, Cassie thought, but she couldn't seem to stop the regrets from adding up until she felt smothered by them.

"Oh, God, how can I do it?" she murmured, hands over her face. And suddenly the tears she had refused to give in to in front of Cole cascaded down her cheeks.

That was how her mother found her, still leaning against the door, sobbing as if her heart would break.

"What on earth?" Edna said, hurrying to her daughter's side. "Cassie, what happened? Is it Jake? Is he hurt?"

Only the very real panic in her mother's voice snapped her out of her desolation. "No, no, Mom. Jake is fine. Mildred is baking cookies, and he's over there hoping for samples."

Her mother pressed a hand to her chest. "Thank goodness. You had me scared for a minute. Now come on over here and sit down and tell me what has you so upset. I woke up from my nap and heard you in here crying."

Cassie followed her mother to the sofa, but when she was seated she couldn't seem to make herself explain what had happened. Her mother would blame herself that it had come to this, and she didn't need the stress.

"Cassie?"

"I just saw Cole," she said finally.

"He's back, then. How is he?"

"Still furious."

"That was to be expected. He'll calm down soon enough, and then you two can deal with this rationally."

"I think it's too late for that," Cassie said ruefully.

Her mother's gaze narrowed. "Oh?"

"He expects me to marry him."

Even her mother gasped at that. "Now? After all that's happened?" Her expression brightened just a little. "Has he forgiven you, then?"

"Hardly. He says it's that or a custody fight." She sighed. "Not exactly the proposal of a lifetime, is it?"

"What is he thinking? That's absurd. He can't make you do that."

"Can't he?"

"What did you tell him?"

"That I would give him an answer on Sunday."

"You're not seriously considering this, are you? I know you still have feelings for him, and I honestly believe he has feelings for you, but the timing couldn't be worse. You need to work through your differences before you even consider getting married."

"I don't think Cole is interested in working through anything," Cassie said honestly. "He wants his son. This is his way of getting him. I just happen to be part of the package. He's willing to put up with me."

"I don't believe that. The man loves you. He can't admit it to himself right now, but he will forgive you. He just needs some time."

"If I believed that, then it wouldn't be so hard to say yes, but, Mom, what if you're wrong? What if he really does hate me? What if he can't forgive me? How can we possibly live under the same roof?"

"You can't and that's that," her mother said grimly. "You'll just have to stall him until you can figure out how he really feels."

"I don't think Cole is in any mood for my stalling tactics. He pretty much said I either do this his way or I take my chances in court."

"Have you talked to Emma? She's in town, isn't she?"

Cassie nodded. Emma had come back to take a controversial case that no lawyer in town would touch. Just last week Cassie had gotten the impression that no matter how that case went, Emma might be back to stay.

"I'll call her first thing in the morning," she said.

"Call her now," her mother urged. "It's not that late, and you won't sleep a wink if you don't get some answers tonight."

"You're right," she agreed, and went into the kitchen to call.

Emma sounded wide awake when she answered. "Cassie? What's wrong? You sound like you've been crying."

"It's been a difficult evening," she said, putting it mildly. "Do you have a few minutes?"

"For you? Of course. What's this about?"

"Custody of Jake."

"I'm coming over," Emma said at once.

"You don't have to..." Cassie began, but she was wasting her breath.

"I'm on my way," Emma said, then hung up before Cassie could argue.

Cassie looked up to meet her mother's worried frown. "She's on her way."

"Good. I'm sure she'll have sensible advice."

"I don't need sensible," Cassie said. "I need the advice of a legal shark who takes no prisoners."

Her mother managed a faint grin. "Then you've called the right person. Our Emma didn't earn her reputation in Denver by being anybody's patsy."

Cassie was startled by the observation. "How do you know so much about her reputation in Denver?"

"Ever since she took that case here, the paper's been running stories about how tough she is. I have to admit I was surprised. When you were girls, you gave her an awful lot of grief, and she took it without so much as a whimper."

"Maybe that's what toughened her up," Cassie said. She was beginning to feel the first little hint of optimism by the time the doorbell rang. Emma swept in with eyes blazing and a determined jut to her jaw. She gave Cassie a fierce hug, then plunked her briefcase on the dining room table and pulled out a chair.

"Start at the beginning. I want to know everything Cole said to you."

As Cassie talked, Emma took notes, never once flinching, not even when Cassie summed up that night's conversation and the proposal that was Cole's alternative to a custody battle. When Cassie had concluded, Emma sighed and rubbed her eyes.

"We can give him a fight, if that's what he wants," she said, then clasped Cassie's hand. "But I won't lie to you, he has a good case. I don't think he could get sole custody of Jake, but he could certainly get visitation rights and perhaps even some form of joint custody. You have absolutely no grounds for accusing him of being unfit, especially since he never had a chance to demonstrate his parenting skills."

Cassie drew in a deep breath. "Then I have no choice. I have to marry him."

"That's up to you, of course." She touched Cassie's cheek. "It doesn't have to be a fate worse than death, you know. You do love him."

"A lot of good that does."

Emma smiled. "Not that you could prove it by me, but I've heard that love can perform miracles."

"Well, I'm certainly about to put it to the test, aren't I?"

Cole took a room in a hotel while he awaited Cassie's decision. When news of his return reached his father, Frank Davis came striding into the hotel lobby demanding to see him. At the commotion just outside the door to the hotel coffee shop, Cole glanced up from behind his newspaper and sighed.

"Over here, Dad," he said.

His father crossed the small lobby and headed straight for his table. He sank down opposite Cole. "It's about time you got back here. Why aren't you at the ranch?"

"Do you even have to ask?"

"Are you planning on staying in this place?" his father asked, glancing around at the shabby furnishings, the tiny coffee shop that had only a handful of scarred tables.

"That depends."

"On?"

"What happens this Sunday."

His father regarded him with exasperation. "Stop talking in riddles. Are you back here to stay or not?"

"I'll keep you posted."

For just an instant his father looked older than his years. He looked defeated. "I suppose I might as well put the ranch on the market. I can't manage it anymore on my own."

Cole scowled at him. "Don't pull that with me. You recovered from that heart attack years ago. You could run the whole state if you were of a mind to, never mind one little cattle ranch."

"Fifty thousand acres isn't little," his father said heatedly. "It's a demanding job, and I just don't have the heart for it anymore. Not if there's no one to leave it to."

"Leave it to your grandson."

"How am I supposed to do that? The boy doesn't even know we're related. If it's left up to his mother, he never will."

"That will change," Cole said grimly. One way or another.

"Oh?" His father's expression brightened. "You going after custody?"

"No. Not the way you mean, anyway."

"What then?"

"I'll tell you on Sunday." He would know how this was going to play out by then.

His father struggled to his feet, looking disgusted. "You're wasting time, Son. I would have had this settled long ago."

"Probably so," Cole agreed. "But for once I'm doing things my way."

And they'd better work out, he thought, or he'd never hear the end of it.

For once Cassie wished the preacher's sermon would go on and on. Instead, Pastor Kirkland spoke for only a few minutes, citing the late-August heat and lack of air-conditioning as the reason for his brevity.

"No point in talking if no one can hear me over the fluttering of those fans you're waving," he said. "You can all give thanks to the Lord for that and we'll call it a day."

The congregation laughed appreciatively, sang one final, rousing hymn, then began to file out. Cassie was one of the last to go. When she reached the church steps, she spotted Cole at once, leaning against the fender of his car, his eyes shaded by sunglasses and the brim of his Stetson.

"You've made up your mind, then?" her mother asked, clinging to her hand. "There's nothing I can say to change it?"

"Nothing," Cassie said grimly. "This is what I have to do."

As she crossed the street, she wished she could feel one tiny little surge of joy, one little spark of hope, but Cole's somber expression wasn't encouraging. He was there to make a deal, not a love match.

He opened the car door for her without speaking, then got into the driver's side and started the engine. He glanced her way once, then focused on the road. Not until they were parked in a secluded spot along the river did he face her.

"Well?"

"I'll do it," she said. "I'll marry you."

He responded with little more than a nod of satisfaction. "Will next weekend suit you?"

Cassie bit back a cry of dismay. What had she thought, that he would allow her time to plan something lavish? Had she honestly expected him to let her carry out the charade that this was the wedding of her dreams, the start of a happy life for two people deeply in love?

"Fine," she said tersely.

"At the church or at town hall?"

Cassie didn't think she could bear either one. "At home, in the garden," she said, ready to fight for that much at least. "I'll speak to Pastor Kirkland about it."

"What time?"

She had always dreamed of a wedding at sunset with color splashed across the western sky. "Seven-thirty," she said, allowing herself this one romantic touch, even if it would mean nothing at all to the man beside her. She hesitated, then asked, "Will you be inviting your father?"

Cole nodded. "I can't see any way around it."

"Anyone else?"

"No."

"I'll want my friends there."

"Whatever," he said, looking completely uninterested in the details now that the decision had been made.

It seemed as if there was nothing else to discuss, not about the ceremony itself, anyway. But there was one thing—the most important thing—that couldn't be ignored.

"Cole, how do I explain this to Jake?"

His hands tightened on the steering wheel until his knuckles turned white. "Why not try the truth? It's about time, don't you think?"

"He's nine. He won't understand the truth, not all of it, anyway."

Cole sighed. "No, I suppose not." He turned slightly toward her, removed his sunglasses and met her gaze directly for the first time all afternoon. "He needs to know I'm his father. We can tell him together, if you'd like."

She nodded. "That would be good, I think. And I want him to know that we loved each other back then," she said fiercely, regarding Cole defiantly, prepared to fight for that, too. "I don't want him to think for a single second that he was a mistake. Nor do I want him to figure out that this marriage is nothing more than a bargain I made with the devil."

"The devil, am I? I've been called worse." For an instant Cole's expression softened. "I suppose it won't be much of a lie, telling him that we loved each other. Back then what we had was pretty special."

Her heart flipped over at the wistfulness in his voice. "Do you think…? Can we get that back again?"

He didn't answer right away. Eventually he slid his sunglasses back into place and looked away. "I honestly don't know," he said in a voice devoid of emotion.

Determined now, she put her hand on his arm, felt his muscle jerk beneath her touch. "We have to try, Cole," she said urgently. "For Jake's sake, if not our own."

Cole's only response was to reach for the key and start the car, his gaze straight ahead. His silence told her all she needed to know. He was nowhere close to forgiving her. In fact, it seemed as if he might not even intend to try.

Saturday dawned under a blazing sun. As wedding days went, Cole supposed this one was picture perfect, but there was none of the joy he'd once expected, none of the anticipation. In fact, all he felt was an aching sense of loneliness, accompanied by the certainty that a few words spoken today at sunset were unlikely to alter that feeling in any way.

Refusing to dwell on his dark mood, he spent the morning working at his computer, then headed for Cassie's. To her mother's dismay, they had dismissed the traditional superstition about the groom not seeing his bride before the wedding and agreed that today was the perfect time to tell Jake the truth about Cole being his father. At least he would have a few hours to get used to the idea before the ceremony. Cole also intended to ask his son to be his best man.

When he arrived at the house, he was surprised by the whirl of activity going on. Flowers and chairs were being carried into the backyard, a small tent was being set up with tables beneath it. Lauren, wearing shorts, a

T-shirt and rollers in her hair, was directing traffic. Cole grinned despite himself.

"You'd better hope there are no paparazzi around," he teased. "The tabloids would pay a fortune for this picture. You are not at your glamorous best."

"If you only came over here to harass me and get in the way, you can leave," she said, frowning at him. "Why anybody would insist on having a wedding in less than a week is beyond me."

"We didn't want a lot of hoopla," he said defensively, aware that she must not know the whole story.

"Maybe you didn't, but Cassie deserves a lot of hoopla, and, by golly, she's going to have as much of it as we can pull off on short notice."

Cole withstood the icy glint in her eyes and the barely concealed criticism. One of the things he'd always admired about Lauren and the others was their fierce loyalty to each other. He'd never had friends like that...except for Cassie. Somewhere along the way, through no fault of his own, he'd lost that. Among the regrets in his life, that one was right at the top of the list.

He sighed at the thought and went in search of his bride-to-be. He found her in the kitchen getting a manicure. Pink flooded her cheeks when he walked in, but Gina barely spared him a glance.

"You're not supposed to be here," she said, and went right on painting Cassie's neatly filed nails a pale shade of pink.

Cassie cleared her throat. "Actually, he is. We're supposed to talk to Jake, explain things."

"Well, you can't do it now," Gina said briskly. "I'm not finished." She waved Cole away. "Go in the living room or out back and make yourself useful. I'll let you know when she's free.''

Cassie shrugged. ''Better do as she says. I've given up fighting with them.''

Amused despite himself, he nodded. ''Yes, I can see why it would be a waste of breath. Where's Jake?''

''Hiding out in his room, if he's smart,'' she said dryly. ''Lauren brought him a tuxedo.''

So that's the way it was going to be, then, Cole concluded. They were going to make this wedding into a special occasion for Cassie's sake, or die trying.

''I'll look for him,'' he said.

Alarm flared in Cassie's eyes. ''You won't say anything, though, not till I can get up there?''

''No,'' he promised. ''I won't say anything.''

He found Jake in his room, staring not at the computer screen as Cole had expected, but out the window at the frenzied activity down below. He glanced up when Cole came in, but his expression was bleak.

''Hey, kiddo,'' Cole said, joining him at the window. ''What's up?''

''You and Mom are gonna get married today, right?''

''That's right.'' Something in Jake's voice alerted him that the boy found the news troubling in some way. He studied him intently, then asked, ''Is that okay with you?''

''I guess,'' Jake said, then regarded Cole with a serious expression. ''How come I didn't know anything about it till practically the last minute?''

''That's when we decided,'' Cole said. ''I thought you might be happy about it.''

He regarded Cole earnestly. ''I think it's pretty cool that you're going to be around all the time,'' he admitted, then added, ''but there's something I don't get.''

''What's that?''

''Nobody seems really excited, not even Mom. In fact, she looks kinda sad.''

Cole winced. ''I think maybe it's just a little overwhelming,'' he said. ''It all happened so fast, and there was a lot to do.''

''But Grandma keeps crying. I heard her tell Mom that this was all her fault.'' His brow puckered with a frown. ''But I don't know what that means. How can having a wedding be anybody's fault?''

Cole put his hands on the boy's shoulders and gave him a reassuring squeeze. ''It's just some grown-up stuff. It's nothing for you to worry about, pal.''

''You love my mom, though, right? I mean that's why you're getting married, isn't it?''

Cole closed his eyes against the tide of pain that that innocent question sent through him. There was no easy answer. A part of him, a part he had worked like the dickens to bury, did love Cassie.

''Yes,'' he said, giving Jake the answer he needed to hear, even if it was only half-true, even if the whole truth was far more complicated. If he couldn't understand it, how could this nine-year-old boy?

Jake nodded, looking relieved. ''I thought so.'' Suddenly he threw his arms around Cole and hugged him. ''I can't wait till we're a real family.''

Cole sighed. Would the bond being formed a few hours from now ever be that clear and that simple?

''Cole, can I ask you something else?''

''Anything, pal.''

''Do you think maybe I could have a baby brother?

I guess it wouldn't be my real brother, but almost, right? That would be so cool. I'd even take a sister.''

For the first time since he'd put this plan into motion, Cole realized the full ramifications. Jake, if no one else, was expecting a real marriage, complete with brothers and sisters. How in heaven's name was he supposed to get around that? For the last week he'd been moving ahead with caution, taking one day at a time. Now with a single innocent question Jake had forced him to gaze into the future.

''I think maybe we'd better discuss that another time,'' Cole said, aware that his voice sounded vaguely choked up. He cleared his throat. ''It's a little soon to be talking about babies.''

He heard Cassie's muffled gasp and realized she had arrived just in time to hear his comment. Even out of context, she had obviously guessed the general direction of the conversation.

''It certainly is,'' she said, stepping into the room and giving Cole a questioning look.

''Jake's looking ahead.''

''Obviously.'' She sat on the edge of the bed and beckoned her son over. ''Sit with me. We want to talk to you.''

Jake went to her readily. ''What about?''

''There's something you need to know before Cole and I get married today.'' Her gaze sought Cole's and held. ''A long time ago he and I were very good friends.''

''When you were kids, right?'' Jake asked.

''Exactly. We were very young and for a long time we were just good friends, but then we fell in love.''

Jake's eyes widened. ''Really?''

''That's right,'' Cole said. ''But then some things

happened and we were separated. I didn't know that
your mom was having a baby."

"You mean me," Jake guessed.

"Exactly." He took a deep breath, then added, "I
didn't know that she was going to have my son."

For a minute Cole's words hung in the air. Jake
looked from Cole to his mother and back again, a puzzled look on his face.

"Cole is your father," Cassie explained quietly.
"But he never knew that until a few weeks ago."

Cole reached out to touch his son's cheek, but pulled
back before making contact. "Nothing could have
made me happier, Jake. I am very proud that you're
my boy."

Jake swallowed hard, clearly struggling to compre-
hend the announcement. "You're my real dad?" he
whispered at last. He looked at Cassie. "He is? For
real?"

She nodded. "He really is."

"Oh, wow," Jake said, awestruck. "Then we really
are gonna be a family. I'm gonna have my mom *and*
my dad." He bounced up. "Does Grandma know? I've
gotta tell her."

He raced out the door, then turned around and ran
back, throwing himself at Cole before taking off again.

Cole met Cassie's gaze and allowed himself a faint
smile. "He seems to be taking it well."

"You've just made his dream come true. He's finally
got his real dad in his life."

But, gazing into her despondent eyes, Cole had to
ask himself if the price he and Cassie were paying for
uniting Jake's family was too high.

Chapter Thirteen

The ceremony went off without a hitch. Cassie actually managed to say her vows around the lump in her throat. She hadn't been able to meet Cole's gaze, though. It would have been too hard to look in his eyes and not see the love shining there that every bride had a right to expect on her wedding day. Just thinking about what was lacking had her blinking back tears as the minister pronounced them man and wife.

Then there was that awkward moment when Pastor Kirkland had announced that Cole could kiss the bride. She had stood there waiting, panicked that he would refuse and embarrass them both. But finally he had lowered his head and touched his lips to hers. It hadn't been a passionate kiss, but it had lingered, and there had been heat in it, more than she'd had any right to expect.

Her friends made every effort to pretend that this

was a perfectly normal wedding. Lauren had outdone herself to turn the garden into a perfect setting. She had had exotic flowers flown in, along with a designer wedding dress. Cassie had almost wept when she'd seen the delicate lace and organza confection. Never in her wildest dreams had she ever imagined wearing such a gown.

But then, never in her wildest dreams had she imagined a wedding day that was such a sham.

Not that anyone was acknowledging that. Everyone was painfully polite, determinedly upbeat. Frank Davis was acting as if he'd been looking forward to Cassie's marriage to his son for years. Her mother's tears could be dismissed as typical of the mother of the bride. If her proud smile seemed a little forced, no one commented on it. And exhilarated by the discovery that Cole was his real father, Jake scooted from one guest to another to share that incredible news.

Meanwhile, her friends were offering up toasts with French champagne and snapping pictures as she and Cole cut the gorgeous three-tiered wedding cake that Lauren had had flown in from Beverly Hills along with the caterer himself. The man had moaned when he'd seen her mother's kitchen, then gone to work whipping up the most amazing hors d'oeuvres under Gina's watchful gaze. Though Gina grumbled at not being allowed to do the job herself, Cassie noted that she seemed happy enough taking surreptitious notes on the recipes. It was the first interest she'd shown in anything related to her restaurant business since arriving in Winding River weeks ago.

Studying the small gathering, Cassie concluded that everyone except the bride and groom seemed to be having a blast. They were all happily caught up in the llusion of happily-ever-after that weddings always evoked.

When she could stand it no longer, she went looking for her new husband. She found him all alone on the front porch, an untouched glass of champagne dangling from his fingers and an unreadable expression on his handsome face.

"Quite a day," he said without looking up when she joined him.

"It was a dream wedding," she said, unable to keep the wistful note out of her voice. If only the bride and groom had been happy, she thought.

"Yeah, too bad it was such a farce, huh?"

Hearing him voice it hurt as badly as being a part of the subterfuge. Some part of her had obviously been hoping against hope that the occasion, or maybe the wedding vows themselves, would soften his attitude, that he would want all of this to be real.

"I need to get out of here," she said stiffly. "I don't think I can bear it for another second."

"Anxious for your wedding night?" he taunted.

She swallowed hard and fought tears. "Hardly." In fact, she hadn't anticipated a wedding night at all. She was positive that Cole intended this to be a marriage in name only, if only to punish her. Maybe even to punish himself for being foolish enough to marry her.

He glanced at her. "I've arranged for you to have your own suite at the hotel until we decide what we're going to do," he said, confirming her guess and stripping away any lingering hope she might have harbored that it would be otherwise.

She stared at him blankly. "What we're going to do?" she repeated. "What does that mean?"

"Whether we're going to leave Winding River," he

explained. "I can set up shop in California or anywhere else, for that matter."

The explanation—the very prospect of leaving—was too much. The thought of running away once more, essentially in disgrace—even if she was the only one who understood that—was overwhelming. She bounced off the swing.

"I am not leaving here," she said, scowling down at him. "I've gone along with everything you wanted, but not that."

He didn't seem the least bit disconcerted or distressed by her vehemence. "I just thought it might be easier to start fresh in a new place, where no one knows our history. We'd be just like any other couple who's grown apart. No one would know we'd never really been together in the first place."

"No, Cole," she said, standing up to him on this as she hadn't on anything else. "We did this to give Jake a family. That means a whole family, including your father and my mother."

"Heaven help the kid," he said grimly, but he nodded. "Okay, then, we stay. You can start looking for a house tomorrow."

"I gather you don't want to live at the Double D?"

"Not a chance."

She breathed a sigh of relief. The prospect of living under Frank Davis's thumb had been daunting. Maybe she and Cole would have half a chance to work things out if they were on their own.

"In town? Or would you prefer a ranch?" she asked.

"Not a ranch," he said at once. "Though buying some property outside of town and building would be okay. That way we'll get exactly what we want, a place with plenty of room."

So they would barely have to speak, much less spend time together? she wondered. How had it come to this? How could there be such a terrible distance between two people who had once shared everything? Of course, the answer was plain enough. She was responsible. She had no one to blame but herself for destroying the trust that they had once felt.

"Building would take time," she pointed out, even though her imagination was already at work on all the possibilities. She wondered if he even remembered that once upon a time they had spun their fantasies about what their dream house would look like. It had been spacious but cozy, with lots of fireplaces, overstuffed furniture and a king-size bed for the two of them. That bed had been the centerpiece of all their daydreams. Her cheeks burned at the memory. Now there would be separate beds, separate rooms, if Cole had his way.

"We have the time," he said, his gaze locked with hers.

For a heartbeat she thought she saw affection, at least, in his eyes, maybe a promise that as the weeks and months passed, they would work things out.

Then he had to go and ruin it by lifting his champagne glass and adding in a sarcastic tone, "After all, isn't this the first day of the rest of our lives?"

Deliberate cruelty had never been in Cole's nature. As he heard himself taunting Cassie repeatedly on their wedding day, he wondered if this new pattern of behavior was tapping into an uncontrollable dark side of him, a side far too much like his father in the early days after his mother's death. He hated the hurt that darkened her eyes, hated that he was responsible, but once his bitterness had been unleashed, he hadn't been able to stop.

Cassie's mother had insisted on keeping Jake with her for a few days while Cole and Cassie settled into married life. Obviously, she was determined to keep up the charade that this was a real marriage. And because he cared about her, had always cared about her, he let her have her illusions. He even went so far as to take Cassie's hand as they ran to the car that her friends had decorated with painted slogans and strings of empty cans.

At the hotel, though, he left Cassie at the door to her adjoining suite, then retreated to the bar, where he nursed a drink and his dark thoughts for hours.

This was the part he hadn't considered when he'd made his impulsive decision to marry her rather than fight her for custody of his son. He hadn't imagined what it would be like to know that Cassie was upstairs, dressed in something slinky and sexy, perhaps, wondering if there was to be a real wedding night. He hadn't thought ahead to how it would feel to know that she was his wife, that legally, at least, they were bound together.

He muttered a harsh expletive and tossed some money on the bar, then headed upstairs. Until he reached the door to his own room, he'd thought he was going to bed—alone. But that image of Cassie wearing lace wouldn't quit, and his body didn't seem to understand that she was the enemy, the betrayer.

He took a few steps toward her door, then backtracked to his own, then cursed himself for a fool. He went back to hers and hammered on it.

"Yes?"

Her voice was muffled and sleepy and so damn sexy
it made his blood roar.

"It's me," he said tightly.

She opened the door and destroyed his illusions. She
was wearing an oversize T-shirt that skimmed her
knees. Her hair was rumpled, her cheeks streaked with
dried tears, her eyes filled with distress. All the same,
she was so blasted desirable it made him ache.

If she'd been waiting for him, though, she had long
since given up. Cole raked a hand through his hair and
bit back another curse.

Still, she was his wife now...if he dared to claim
her. He thought about it, then sighed, defeated by his
own conscience.

"Sorry," he mumbled. "I thought you might be
awake."

"I was until a few minutes ago," she said. "Do you
want to come in?"

"No," he said, then, "Yes."

A faint smile touched her lips, then faded. "Can't
make up your mind?"

"I shouldn't be here."

"Why not? We *are* married. I have a paper that says
so."

"Yeah, but we both know..." His voice trailed off.

"What? That it's not real?"

He nodded. What amazed him right now, though,
was that it felt real, even though it wasn't supposed to.
He wanted her. He wanted all the things they had once
talked about...a future, a family, a home. He wanted
to make love to Cassie Collins Davis and prove that
she was finally his.

He gazed into her eyes, saw the little spark of desire,
caught the way her lips parted as if she was about to

speak...or about to welcome his kiss. He steeled himself against his own traitorous desire and took a step back.

"I'm sorry. I shouldn't have disturbed you," he said stiffly.

"Cole—"

"No, Cassie. I am not coming in there." He said it as if she were the one who'd set out to tempt him, rather than take responsibility for his own actions in coming to her door.

"Then why are you here?"

"I wish to God I knew."

She nodded at that. The hope that had been in her eyes dimmed, then died. Her expression hardened. "Then do me a favor," she said quietly. "Don't come back until you do."

He wanted to argue that she was his wife and that he'd damn well come and go as he pleased, but what was the point? She was right. He had no business being here, not unless he was willing to forgive and forget, and he was far from ready to do that. He wasn't sure he would *ever* be able to do that.

But as he turned and walked away, as he heard the whisper of her sigh as the door clicked shut behind him, he wondered if he hadn't just consigned them both—not just her, but the two of them—to a life of pure hell.

Cassie hadn't thought it was possible to be any more miserable than she had been waiting for Cole to decide what he wanted from her, but she'd been wrong. This so-called marriage was worse. Much worse.

To be so close to a man she loved and know that he didn't trust her, that, in fact, he all but hated her, was sheer torment. Whatever hope she had felt when he'd held her in his arms just a few short weeks ago at the reunion dance was gone. The hunger and heat stirred by his touch was little more than cold ashes now. All of it had been lost due to her years of deceit.

The day after the wedding she got up, got dressed and waited for some sign from Cole of what he expected. When he hadn't come by nine, she ordered breakfast in her room. She was tempted to change clothes and go to work, but Stella would have been appalled, and tongues all over town would have wagged. Cassie felt the same way about going to church. To arrive alone on the morning after her wedding would have stirred all sorts of comment.

By noon, though, she was going stir-crazy. Grabbing her keys, she went downstairs, got in her car and headed for Karen's. If ever there was a time to be with her best friends, this was it.

She found all four Calamity Janes seated around the kitchen table debating the merits of various gourmet coffees. Well, Lauren and Gina were debating them, anyway. Karen and Emma were exchanging amused looks. All of them looked up, clearly startled, as Cassie walked in.

"Any of that coffee left for me?" she asked as if her arrival was nothing out of the ordinary. "And I don't care what kind it is, as long as it's strong."

Karen jumped up, pulled out a chair for her and poured the coffee, as the others simply stared.

"Stop it," Cassie ordered. "I haven't grown two heads overnight, have I?"

"It's just a surprise," Gina began cautiously. "You got married yesterday. I thought—we all thought..."

"Well, you thought wrong," she said succinctly.

"Where's Cole?"

Cassie shrugged. "Beats me. I haven't seen him since last night."

Emma scowled. "The man walked out on you right after your wedding night?"

"Only in the loosest interpretation of that," Cassie said mildly. "Technically there was no wedding night. And he never walked in, much less out."

Gina clasped her hand. "Explain," she ordered. "Then we can go strangle him."

Cassie opened her mouth, but the words wouldn't come. Instead, all the hurt and humiliation bubbled up from deep inside. Great choking sobs emerged, taking her and the rest of them by surprise.

For an instant her friends just sat there. Then they were all around her, patting her back, handing her tissues and describing Cole in such unflattering terms that eventually even Cassie began to smile.

"He is not meaner and uglier than a hound dog," she said, sniffing. "That's the trouble. I'm only getting what I deserve."

"Don't be absurd," Emma snapped. "You don't deserve to be treated like this, abandoned on your wedding night."

"You, of all people, know why we got married. This wasn't a love match."

"Oh, of course it was," Lauren retorted, haughtily dismissing the claim. "And the sooner the two of you realize it, the sooner you can get on with the business of being married. Cole's just being bullheaded."

"I lied to him," Cassie reminded her.

"And you've apologized. Jake's in his life now. Cole needs to get over the past and move on."

"Otherwise, I'll be down at the courthouse first thing tomorrow filing for an annulment," Emma threatened.

"I think I'm the one who'd have to do that," Cassie teased, amazed at how much better she felt knowing these women were on her side. That they knew the whole story—or most of it—and loved her anyway.

Emma frowned. "You know what I meant. He is not going to get away with tormenting you."

Karen, silent up until now, reached for Cassie's hand. "Do you still love him?" she asked quietly.

"Of course I do," she said without hesitation. Only in the past few days with misery building at the distance between them had she realized just how much.

"Have you told him that?"

"Not in so many words."

"Why not?"

"Because he'd throw the words back in my face."

Karen shook her head. "I don't think so—but so what if he does? You just keep saying 'em till he gets the message. Don't let pride stand in your way, Cassie. Life is too short to waste a single second of it."

The message was powerful enough on its own, but coming from Karen, who'd so recently lost her beloved husband, it carried additional weight.

"Talk to him," Karen insisted. "And do it now. Hanging around here with us isn't solving your problem."

Cassie wasn't so sure about that. Being here with her friends had given her a sense of peace. Karen's advice had solidified her resolve to make this marriage work. She stood up and gave each of her friends a hug.

"You guys are the best," she said. "I knew if I came here I'd feel better."

"Now go back there and give him hell," Emma said.

"Tell him you love him," Karen corrected, poking Emma in the ribs.

Emma sighed. "Whatever. But call me if you want to nail the guy's hide in court."

"Emma, you really do have to learn to express yourself less subtly," Gina teased. "No one can ever figure out what you're thinking."

"Emma's just a passionate defender of the underdog," Lauren said. "There's nothing wrong with that. It's why she's so good in court. Now leave her alone."

"Yeah, leave me alone," Emma said. "I'm not the same little wimp you guys used to walk all over."

"Really?" Gina asked with exaggerated shock.

Cassie chuckled at all the bantering and left Karen's with her heart lighter and her determination renewed. No matter how long it took, she was going to win Cole's heart again.

Unfortunately, as the first weeks of her marriage crept by with no thawing of Cole's attitude, Cassie slowly sank into despair again. Though the three of them—she, Cole and Jake—frequently shared meals, Cole made it a point never to be alone with her. Their conversations were limited to plans for the house and anything concerning their son. He didn't discuss his work or his days, and he never asked about hers. The wall between them was getting thicker and thicker with each passing week. She began to think it would take a wrecking ball to break it down.

Thankfully, though, Cole's chilly attitude didn't extend to Jake. The time he spent with his son, making up for all the lost years, was the only thing that kept Cassie going. Their bond was growing stronger day by day, and Jake was flourishing with all of the male attention.

Coming back to the hotel after her shift at Stella's, which she had refused to give up, she glanced into Cole's office and saw them, their heads bent over the computer keyboard. Jake was peppering Cole with a thousand questions, which he answered with an endless supply of patience.

Cassie sighed heavily. Would her own relationship with her husband ever reach that stage again? Would there ever be the easy camaraderie they'd once shared? Only one thing gave her any hope at all. Despite Cole's cold attitude, she could tell that he still wanted her. From time to time she caught him watching her, his gaze hooded. On occasion he reached out, as if to touch her, only to withdraw without making contact. It was evident that the embers of their passion hadn't entirely cooled.

Even without Karen's advice still ringing in her ears, she knew she had a choice to make. She could endure this marriage and keep her pride, or she could risk her heart to change it. She had opted for pride once and nearly lost everything. This time she wouldn't make the same mistake.

Sex wasn't love, but it was a means of communication, an undeniable form of intimacy, of sharing. Slowly she would turn Cole's desire into need.

And over time she prayed she could turn it into love.

Chapter Fourteen

Cassie was driving Cole crazy. First there had been the constant hurt in her eyes, which left him filled with guilt.

Then there'd been unmistakable signs of anger. That had stiffened his resolve, prepared him for a battle that hadn't come.

Now lately she had been doing everything in her power to seduce him. The changes were keeping him dizzy and off balance, wavering between guilt and yearning.

He'd tried telling himself that this last, sly attempt to seduce was merely wishful thinking on his part, but there was no mistaking the intent of her glancing touches, the subtle perfume, the suddenly provocative attire on a woman who'd always preferred denim to lace. She wanted him and she intended to get him, by fair means or foul.

And he, blast it all, was losing the battle. How could he hold out against a woman he'd spent the past ten years wanting?

"Cole?"

"Hmm?" he responded distractedly. When she stroked his cheek with a lingering caress, his gaze shot up. Where had she come from? She rarely entered his room without knocking, but here she was, lips moist, color high. He eyed her suspiciously. "What?"

"Do you have a minute?" she asked, her expression all innocence as her hand fell away.

She was wearing white shorts and some skimpy little triangle of fabric that pretended to be a blouse. Aside from a few bows holding it all together, her back was bare, as were her feet. Rather than her usual pale-pink, she had painted her toenails a kick-ass-red. Staring down at those erotic little toes, he lost his train of thought completely.

"Cole, do you have a minute?" she repeated, amusement threading through her voice.

"I suppose," he said uneasily. "Is there a problem with Jake?"

"No. He's fine. He's spending the night with my mother. He won't be back till after lunchtime tomorrow."

Uh-oh, he thought. They were alone. She was in his room, not her own, and she was wearing that sexy scent again, the one that made his pulse pound.

"The house?" he asked, sounding a little desperate even to his own ears. He cleared his throat. "Is there a problem with the house? I, um, I could call the contractor." He reached for the phone, clung to it as if it were a lifeline.

She smiled. "Nope. It's coming along right on schedule."

That left what? he wondered, battling panic as he reluctantly set the phone aside. What the dickens did she want? Besides him, of course. Oh, she definitely wanted him, he concluded, meeting her gaze and discovering the heat there.

"Then what's on your mind?" he asked, resigned to a really tough test of his willpower.

She edged closer, sat on the corner of his desk, her gaze locked with his, her very bare thigh nudging his. Even through his own jeans, he could feel the temperature of her skin soar. His body reacted predictably with a rush of blood straight to his groin.

This was a dangerous game she was playing. He wondered if she realized it. One glance into her smoldering eyes answered that. She knew, all right. And she was enjoying every single second of making him sweat, of watching him struggle with himself to do the right thing. She was deliberately trying to blast his conscience right out of the water.

"Cassie?" he prodded, a hitch in his voice.

A purely female smile came and went. "I'm not making you nervous, am I?"

Nervous? Hell, no. He was coming unglued. He was about to go up in flames.

"This..." He cleared his throat yet again. "This isn't wise."

He sounded like a cranky, sixty-year-old prude. Evidently she thought so, too, because she chuckled, a low, throaty sound that danced down his spine like a flame.

"Really? Why not?"

"Do I really have to explain it?"

She regarded him thoughtfully for a second, then nodded. "Yes, I think you do."

"Because we have issues," he began, then all but groaned. Not a sixty-year-old prude. Maybe ninety—and a stiff-necked psychiatrist to boot.

She nodded, acknowledging what he said, but she didn't look swayed. Nor did she budge one millimeter away from his thigh.

"Care to talk about them?" she asked, her tone only mildly curious.

Now there was a loaded question, if ever he'd heard one. If he said yes, he would be opening up the whole blasted can of worms he'd been trying so hard to ignore. If he said no, he was pretty sure she had some other way for them to spend the time.

He swallowed hard, cleared his throat, then shrugged. "What's the point?" he asked, proud of himself for coming up with a third option, an evasion that might annoy her enough to convince her to leave.

"Oh, I don't know. It might clear the air," she said, sounding amused perhaps, but definitely not annoyed.

He, however, was getting downright irritable. Her attitude was exasperating. Her proximity was arousing. The conflicting messages were roaring around in his head...and elsewhere.

"It. Would. Not. Clear. The. Air." He bit the words out from between clenched teeth.

She swung her legs, deliberately letting her calf brush his. "Oh, I don't know," she said, her expression serious, even thoughtful. "We won't know unless we try."

He narrowed his gaze and studied her. "Is that what you really want?" he asked skeptically. "A nice, polite discussion, a chance to make a few excuses, maybe even some promises?''

A spark of anger flashed in her eyes, and he thought for a second she might really explode, tell him to take his sarcasm and shove it. Instead, she leaned over until her gaze was level with his, until he could feel the soft whisper of her breath against his cheek. His heart raced.

''No,'' she said in that same quiet, intense tone. ''This is what I want.''

Before he could even catch his breath, her mouth was on his, sweet and urgent and hot. Her tongue skimmed his lips, then slid inside, tangling with his. And Cole was pretty sure his entire body was going to go up in flames.

For one tiny, fleeting second, he considered a protest, ordered himself to utter it, in fact, but the moment passed in a frenzy of need. *This* was what he'd missed, *this* was what he and Cassie could be together if only he could let go of his anger and his stiff-necked pride. All it would take was the little matter of forgiving her, of letting go of the past. Right now he was too caught up in the moment to give a hang about anything, the past included.

He groaned and claimed her, deepening the kiss, blanking out all of the arguments against what was happening and seizing the pulse-pounding moment.

She slid into his lap, all willing and eager and hot as a winter fire, just the way he remembered. When he would have moved beyond the devastating kisses for more, she held him still, savoring the mating of their mouths, discovering the amazing nuances possible in a kiss.

His hand drifted to her thigh, skimmed along warm,

supple skin until he reached the core of her heat. He hesitated there, knowing that they were crossing the point of no return. If he touched her intimately, if she let him, there would be no going back. He would have to bury himself inside her. He would have to discover if reality matched fantasy, if the present could equal the memory. He would have to rediscover every texture, every taste, every throbbing response. He would have to make her his.

And he would be hers. Forever. Without denials or recriminations or regrets. Forgiveness might be a struggle for some time to come, but this, *this* would be a given, a habit too hard to break for a second time in his life.

He sighed and held still, waiting for the panic to wash through him, waiting for the anger to resurface and destroy desire. He waited and waited, but it didn't happen.

Instead, anticipation built…along with soul-wrenching need and astonishing heat.

And then she smoothed her hand across his brow as if to wipe away the worry, the distress that had kept him—kept them—from moving on. He was lost, caught up in the magical spell of her touch, in the powerful pull of her tenderness.

"I want you," he admitted at long last. "You have no idea how much I want you."

"I think I do," she soothed, beginning to work the buttons of his shirt.

Her knuckles skimmed lightly across his chest, and then her mouth was there, clever and damp and eager. Her touch turned the wanting to a persistent ache.

Cole thought he might finally understand what it was like to be ravished, to be taken completely and not have the will to fight it, just to go along for the astonishing ride. He was on sensory overload, climbing to a peak that he had no intention of reaching alone.

He reached for Cassie's hands, stilled them, then shifted to evade her lips. "Enough," he commanded, his voice ragged.

Startled smoky eyes met his.

"I am not making love with my wife for the first time since the wedding in an uncomfortable, straight-backed chair," he said, scooping her into his arms and standing up.

He carried her to the bed in the next room. There were a dozen times along the way when he could have allowed sane, sensible thoughts to crowd in and end this, but he ignored everything but the feel of the woman in his arms, the need pounding through his veins.

Tomorrow would take care of itself, he told himself. Tonight was about him and the woman whose memory had burned in his heart for years. If it was all they ever had, he told himself that tonight would be enough.

Cassie hadn't been nearly as sure of herself as she'd wanted Cole to believe. There had been moments, more than she could count, when she'd wanted to dash from his room rather than risk the rejection she feared was coming. Only grim determination and the terror that this might be her one and only chance had kept her there when he'd made it plain he wanted her to go.

Now, as he held her in his arms, as he made steady, deliberate progress toward his bed, she began to allow hope to flare along with desire. Surely this would be the beginning. Surely after tonight the barriers would come down and they would be able to communicate as they once had, as friends *and* as lovers. Not perfectly, not without setbacks, but with the commitment of two people who'd finally figured out what mattered most in their lives.

Inside the room dominated by that great expanse of bed, Cassie felt a moment's triumph. She had gotten them this far. She had taken control of her life—not by running, but by staying. If there had been time, if Cole's clever hands hadn't been busily stripping away her clothes, she would have taken the time to pat herself on the back for finally maturing enough to stay the course, no matter how difficult.

But Cole clearly didn't intend to give her—or himself—time to think. His touches, like hers earlier, were meant to excite. His kisses became deeper and more urgent. When his mouth closed over her breast, a wildfire burst into flame inside her.

This was the way it had been ten years ago—powerful, all-consuming need, frenzied caresses and a buildup so sweet, so intense, that she was sure she would die from it. Instead, just when she thought she could go no higher, when it seemed likely that her body was about to shudder in a wild, cataclysmic release, Cole found some way to ease her down before lifting her back to a new and even higher peak.

Beneath him, she moaned, straining, desperate and awash in sensations, frantic for him to bury himself inside her. His work-roughened hands were gentle, skillful and oh, so devious—tender one second, demanding the next. His muscles, hard from working the ranch, bunched beneath her touch. The body that had invaded her dreams, filling her head with erotic images, was even better in reality. Ten years had added strength and agility, had turned awkward, if delicious, fumbling into skillful lovemaking.

She might have had the will and the incentive to take the initiative tonight, but Cole was in control now, setting the pace, destroying her with his devastating kisses, his tormenting touches. She wanted…she *needed*…

"Cole, please," she begged. "Now. I want you inside me now."

His eyes glittered with satisfaction. His hands cupped her face, and his gaze locked with hers.

Then, oh, so slowly, he entered her at last, sinking deep inside her, filling her. She gasped at the pleasure of it, at the sense of fulfillment that stole over her.

But then he was moving and her body was soaring until together the climbed to the highest peak yet. This time there was no retreat, no blessed relief, just this building urgency, this frantic, fevered yearning that grew hotter and wilder until it exploded through her, then him in shuddering waves.

Cole murmured her name over and over as they clung together, trembling, then slowly…slowly returned to earth…to his bed…to reality.

And to all the problems that couldn't be resolved so easily.

Cassie banished that thought as soon as it dared to creep in. She wouldn't allow it, wouldn't allow anything to spoil this moment. She had waited too long— not just since her wedding night, but years. Illusion or not, she deserved this sweet oblivion.

She sighed and cuddled more tightly against Cole. His arm held her securely, his hand rested on her hip. His breathing grew steadier, whispering against hot, fevered skin, cooling it.

"That was—" she began.

Cole touched a finger to her lips. "Don't say anything."

It was part command, part warning. "Why?" she asked as tension crept in to steal the serenity.

"Just let it be what it was. If we start examining it, things will only get complicated."

Rather than quieting her, the request to leave things be stirred more questions. "Complicated how?"

This time Cole sighed heavily and pulled away, retreating from her not just physically but emotionally. She could feel the sudden chill in the air as surely as if the air-conditioning had kicked on. She gathered the sheet and wrapped herself in it before facing him.

"Cole, talk to me. Don't you dare shut me out now."

"What's the point?"

It wasn't the first time he'd asked that since she'd walked in on him earlier, but it was more devastating now. The hurt and anger she'd been living with for weeks bubbled back to the surface. "The point is that you and I have just made love—using no protection, I might add. We could have made another baby here today."

An expression of such dismay crossed his face that Cassie's heart sank. What she had viewed as a hopeful beginning Cole obviously saw as nothing more than another lapse in judgment. Rather than solving anything, tonight had only complicated their lives, perhaps more than either of them was ready to cope with.

"I assumed you were on the Pill," he said stiffly.

She shivered as ice formed where only moments before there had been fire. "Why would you assume such a thing?" she asked. "I haven't been involved with anyone. You certainly haven't come near me since the wedding. Why would I be on the Pill?''

An unreadable mask slid over his face. ''Because it would be the mature, responsible thing to do if you intended to come into my room and seduce me.''

''And the way you've been behaving is mature?'' she snapped, losing patience. ''You married me, Cole. For better or worse. Did you do it just so you could punish me till the end of time?''

He stiffened at the accusation, but he didn't deny it.

She stared at him incredulously. ''You did, didn't you? Well, I don't intend to live like this.'' She leaped out of the bed and started grabbing clothes and putting them on haphazardly, not worrying with buttons or snaps, just the most basic decency so she could get from his room to her own.

''Oh?'' he said with deadly calm, his gaze hooded as he watched her. ''What will you do? Run?''

''Only across town,'' she said. ''I'll take Jake and—''

''You won't take Jake anywhere,'' he said. ''Jake stays with me.''

''Not until a court says he does,'' she retorted.

He leveled a look at her that might have daunted her if she hadn't been so furious.

''Are you willing to take that chance?'' he asked. ''Are you willing to risk losing your son? I won't go about this halfway. I'll go after full custody.''

She met his gaze and saw that he was absolutely serious. Fury died as fear crept back in. She wouldn't let him see that, though. She couldn't.

''Why do you want to keep me trapped in marriage, Cole? Have you asked yourself that? I think it's because a part of you loves me, a part of you wants to know that I'm yours anytime you get around to forgiving me. You like dangling the prospect of forgiveness in front of me just to torture me, just to get a little revenge for what I did to you.''

He didn't deny any of it, not even her claim that he loved her. He couldn't, because they both knew it was true. The last hour had proved that. More than sex had been involved. They had made love. For a little while anger and hurt had slid away and their hearts had spoken. Cole had wanted this as desperately as she had. He just couldn't make himself admit it.

Cassie might have pitied him for that, but right now she had no pity to spare. She was fighting not just for her son but for her marriage.

"If I stay," she said firmly, her gaze clashing with his, "*if* I stay, then both of us have to work to make this marriage real. We have to do whatever it takes, see a counselor if we can't figure things out on our own. The time has come for drastic measures, Cole. I'm willing." She challenged him with a steady look. "Are you?"

He studied her warily. "Meaning?"

"No more separate bedrooms. No more separate beds." She was adamant about it. There would be no compromise. "I love you. I always have. And I'm sorrier than I can say that I kept your son from you, but the truth is out now. You know. Either we deal with it and move on, together, as a family, or I take Jake and move back in with my mother and we go to court."

Taking such a stance was a risk. She knew it even as the words left her mouth, but she had no choice. She would not live in emotional limbo. Maybe if Cole hadn't mattered to her, she could have done it, but he did matter. He was the love of her life, the father of her son, and the distance between them was killing her bit by bit, day by day. It was worse than when they'd been separated, when she'd thought he had abandoned her.

He gave her a measured look, then said with a degree of bemusement, "You've changed."

"I hope so. I'm not a teenage girl anymore."

"No, I mean in the past few weeks. You're stronger."

Stronger? She wasn't so sure about that. But she did recognize that this was no way to live. If she didn't fight for her future, who would?

"I love you," she said quietly. "If I'm stronger, it's because I've stopped denying that. Maybe there's a lesson in there for you, too. Loving me doesn't make you weak, Cole. It takes a strong man to forgive."

Before he could respond to the challenge of that, she walked out of his room and headed back to her own for what she prayed would be the last time. She would give him until tomorrow to come for her, to say that he was willing to try.

And just in case he stayed stubbornly away, she would begin to pack her bags.

Chapter Fifteen

Cole spent a long, lonely night after Cassie left his bed. He cursed himself for letting it come to this, for weakening his stance, for letting his determination slip.

He debated with himself for hours, wanting one thing, needing another and hating himself because of it. She had betrayed him. She wasn't to be trusted. It was as simple—as black and white—as that.

But it wasn't. It was murky as hell. Maybe there weren't any rights or wrongs. Maybe there wasn't any such thing as justice when emotions were involved. Maybe what was in his heart was all that mattered.

If only he knew precisely what that was. Until today he'd been able to convince himself that he'd married Cassie only so he wouldn't have to fight her for custody of Jake. He'd seen himself as the magnanimous one. Practically a saint, he thought wryly.

But, holding her in his arms, burying himself deep

inside her, he had known better. He was no saint. Far from it. Just as she'd said, he had married her because he couldn't bear the thought of losing her for a second time.

But that was exactly what was going to happen if he didn't get over the anger that ate at him during every waking minute. He'd seen the determination in her eyes last night and again this morning before she'd left for work. She would go, even if that meant a court fight. That she would risk so much proved to him just how serious she was. She wanted all or nothing.

There was only one problem. He wasn't at all sure he could give her what she wanted, not without resentment bubbling up. What chance would they have if it was always there, just below the surface, something to throw in her face whenever they hit a rough patch?

Just let it go, forgive and forget. If he'd asked a half dozen people, five of the six would have told him that was what he needed to do. The sixth would tell him to cling to the anger, to remember it, so she could never hurt him again. That would have been his father's advice—which made it suspect right off.

Frank Davis hadn't let up once since the wedding. Despite the show he'd put on during the reception, he hadn't gone out of his way to welcome Cassie any more than Cole had. He seemed to have forgotten all about his own role in keeping Cassie and his son apart.

At the same time, he was doing everything in his power to turn Jake into the rancher that Cole himself refused to be. It frustrated Frank no end that Jake showed more interest in Cole's computers than he did in cattle.

"You're ruining that boy," Frank grumbled when

he stopped by the hotel the morning after Cole's argument with Cassie and found father and son squinting at the computer screen.

His arrival was a good distraction. It meant Cole wouldn't have to deal with Cassie and the feelings that had come roaring to life the night before. He could ignore them for a little longer, put off having to make the decision he'd spent the night debating.

Jake, unaware of the undercurrents or the depth of his grandfather's disapproval, regarded the older man with innocent excitement. "But this is so cool. Cole's letting me write a real program for a game, one I made up myself. One of these days every kid in America will play it," he said with complete confidence. "Cole said so."

Frank scowled. "What are you doing calling your daddy Cole?" he demanded, seizing on that, rather than commenting on the game that had his grandson so excited.

"Leave it be," Cole said tightly, though it bothered him some, too, that Jake hadn't started calling him Dad.

Jake blinked rapidly at his grandfather's criticism, then gazed up at Cole. "Can I?"

"Can you what?"

"Call you Dad?"

Cole's heart crept into his throat. "Of course you can."

A smile spread across the boy's face. "You never said, so I wasn't sure, and I didn't want to ask Mom, 'cause she looks kinda sad a lot, especially when you and I spend a lot of time together."

"She needs to get over it," Frank grumbled even as Cole shot a warning look in his direction.

"I'll speak to your mother," Cole promised. "I'm sure she won't have any objections." How could she? he thought. There was no denying the relationship. The whole town knew about it by now.

The things he and Cassie needed to discuss were adding up…and most of the topics promised to be uncomfortable.

"Jake, why don't you come out and spend the night at the ranch with me?" Cole's father asked. "That horse I bought for you needs to be ridden."

"I'm not very good," Jake protested.

"And you won't get any better by avoiding it," Frank said.

"Okay, enough," Cole said, frowning at his father. "Don't push him."

"I want to learn to ride," Jake said, regarding his grandfather earnestly. "But that horse is too big, and he doesn't like me."

"Part of learning to ride is learning to control the horse. You'll get the hang of it," Frank insisted.

"Maybe he should start out on Buttercup," Cole said. He grinned at Jake. "She was my first horse."

That was recommendation enough for Jake. "Could I?" Jake begged his grandfather.

"Absolutely," Cole said, not giving his father a chance to refuse or to label the boy a sissy because of his preference for a gentler horse. "Shall I come along?"

"I'm perfectly capable of giving the boy a riding lesson," his father grumbled, clearly understanding Cole's unspoken message. "On Buttercup, if that's the way you want it. The poor old mare can barely make it out of the barn, though."

"Which means she's not likely to run off with him,"

Cole said. He winked at Jake. "Take her an apple, and she'll do whatever you ask of her."

Jake ran to grab one from the basket of fruit the hotel had sent up. "Okay, Grandpa, I'm ready."

Frank looked momentarily taken aback by his eagerness, but he finally gave him a gruff pat on the back. "Let's go, then."

"Jake, shouldn't you get your toothbrush, at least?" Cole asked.

"I don't need one. Grandpa gave me one last time. And there are some jeans and shirts and stuff in my room at the ranch."

Cole regarded his father evenly. "Is that so?"

"No point in having him haul stuff back and forth. He might as well feel at home when he's there."

"Just don't get carried away," he warned his father. He wouldn't put it past the old man to try to convince Jake to move in.

"I have no idea what you mean," Frank retorted, heading for the door at a brisker pace than usual, clearly eager to avoid a drawn-out explanation.

Cole let him leave, then sat back with a sigh and braced himself for Cassie's return from work. He had a decision to make between now and then. He could agree to her terms or go to war. With his body already squarely on her side, in fact eager to join her in bed, the decision was all but made.

He just had to figure out if he could live with it.

Cassie wiped the counter at Stella's with slow, distracted strokes.

"I think it's clean now," Karen commented.

Cassie's gaze shot up. "What?"

She had almost forgotten her friend was there. Karen

had come in right at closing, claiming that she'd had a sudden yearning for a piece of Stella's apple pie. Since Karen's pies had been winning ribbons at the local fair for years now, the explanation hadn't rung true.

Karen placed her hand over Cassie's to still the idle motion. "I said that the counter is clean." Her gaze narrowed. "What's on your mind? Did you and Cole have a fight?"

"We don't exactly fight," Cassie said. "Though yesterday we came as close as we ever have." She sighed. "He's so cool. Even when he's furious with me, he refuses to let down his guard. He just makes some sarcastic comment that's designed to put distance between us."

"Don't let him get away with it," Karen advised. "Call him on it."

"I do. Last night I told him he had to make a decision. We either work at a real marriage or I walk and I take Jake with me."

Karen's eyes widened. "You didn't?"

"What choice did I have? Things are impossible the way they are now. And after yesterday…"

"What happened?"

"We made love," she said, feeling the heat climb into her cheeks at the memory. "And it was the way it used to be—better, in fact."

"That's wonderful. And it's progress." She studied Cassie intently. "So why did you issue an ultimatum after that?"

"Because he would have gone right back to the way things used to be. He was already pulling back even while I was right there next to him."

"He's scared," Karen concluded.

The comment was so ludicrous that Cassie laughed. "Cole Davis isn't scared of anything."

"Sure he is," Karen said. "He's scared of the same thing all men are scared of, letting down their guard and getting hurt. Frankly, I think that's very positive."

"Pardon me if I have a little trouble following your logic. Why is that a good thing?"

"It means he loves you. You still have the power to hurt him and he knows it. It terrifies him. So what does he do? He puts those walls up to protect himself."

Cassie considered the explanation thoughtfully. It made a lot of sense. Unfortunately she wasn't sure how much longer she could fight to try to tear those walls back down. A lot depended on what Cole said when she got back to the hotel today. If he agreed to her terms for staying, they had a chance. If not...

"I don't know what to do anymore," she admitted. "I've tried everything I can think of, including threatening to leave."

"Which would only prove to him that's he's been right all along not to trust you," Karen pointed out.

Well, hell. She was right about that, too. "I can't talk about this anymore. My head is spinning. Let's talk about you. How are you doing?"

"I'm getting through one day at a time," Karen said. "Lauren's been a huge help. She refuses to go away. I feel as if I am totally disrupting her life, but the truth is I'm glad of the company. And she's working as if she's obsessed. She's always had a magic touch with horses, but she's turning into an all-around rancher. I dread the day she goes back to her own life."

Her shoulders slumped and a weary expression settled on her face. "I don't know what I'd do without her. I thought I could do it all, but I can't, and I can't pay for extra help. If I lose the ranch, I'll feel as if I failed Caleb.''

"You're not going to lose the ranch,'' Cassie said fiercely. ''We'll all do whatever it takes to see to that.'' She studied her friend's face. ''Unless, one of these days, you decide there's something you'd rather be doing. If you decide you want to sell, it will be okay, Karen. Caleb would understand.''

"I'm not so sure of that,'' Karen said, then sighed.

"He would,'' Cassie insisted, then gave her friend's hand a squeeze. ''You have to do what's best for you now. And you don't have to decide what that is today or even tomorrow. You take your time. And if you need extra help, call me. I might not be experienced, but I'm willing. And Jake's been learning to do chores at the Double D. He could just as easily do them for you. In fact, I'd prefer it.''

Karen forced a smile. ''Thanks. Now go home to your husband. Your work with me is done.'' Her grin spread. ''And that counter hasn't been that spotless in years, so you're off the hook with Stella, too.''

They walked out of the diner together, then went their separate ways. It wasn't lost on Cassie that both of them were heading home with unmistakable reluctance. There was a difference, though. Karen could never get her husband back, while Cassie still had a fighting chance with hers. Watching her friend climb dejectedly into the battered pickup that had been Caleb's, Cassie resolved to make the most of the chance she had.

Cole looked up when he heard Cassie's key turn in the lock. His pulse ricocheted wildly. This was it, the moment of truth. Do or die. A few more clichés rattled around in his head as he dared to face her, still trying to decide what to say.

"You're home," he said. Now there was a brilliant beginning, he thought, cursing his stupidity. He tried to salvage the moment. "Rough day?"

That was better, he concluded. It sounded like the start of a perfectly normal conversation between husband and wife. Unfortunately, there was nothing normal about any of this. It was awkward as hell.

"It was okay, at least until Karen came in." Her expression turned sad. "I'm worried about her. She's not handling Caleb's death well at all."

"How could she? He's only been gone a few months. It must be a terrible adjustment to make."

"She ought to sell the ranch before it kills her, too," Cassie said. "But right now she won't hear of it. She thinks she owes it to Caleb to stay."

"And as long as she thinks that, then that's what she needs to do," Cole said. "You can't push her. That ranch is her connection to him. It's little wonder she doesn't want to lose that."

Cassie sighed. "I know. Some things can't be rushed."

Her gaze locked with his, and they both knew that she wasn't talking only about Karen. "I'm sorry if I pushed too hard yesterday. I just want...I want things to be okay, to be good between us."

Cole nodded. Here it was, the moment of truth. "I want that, too," he said quietly. "I really do. I'm not saying it can happen overnight, but it is what I want. You need to know that. You need to believe it, even when I'm shutting you out."

"I'll try."

"And sleeping in the same bed will be a start," he added quietly. "If that's something you still want."

Hope lit her eyes. "I do," she said at once. "With all my heart."

"Good."

They stared at each other, neither of them moving, neither of them knowing what else to say, until finally Cole could bear it no longer.

"Come here," he said, beckoning her.

She hesitated.

"Cassie, you're not changing your mind already, are you?"

"No, but—"

"Come here," he commanded.

She took one step toward him, then eventually another, until their knees were touching. He reached up and touched her cheek, surprised to find it was damp with tears he hadn't noticed in the room's shadows.

"Oh, baby," he murmured, drawing her into his lap. "It's going to be okay."

"Is it?" she whispered, sounding more uncertain than he'd ever heard her.

"It is," he said confidently.

Given time, given commitment, given love, it would definitely be okay. Hopefully, he had just bought them the time they needed.

Chapter Sixteen

It wasn't okay, not by a long shot. Oh, Cole was trying. They were sharing a bed, but the gap between them hadn't been closed, not all the way.

Cassie had had high hopes for the move into the new house. Surely then, when they were in the home they'd designed together, the last pieces of their relationship would fall into place. But it wasn't working out that way.

The new house was still not the home she had envisioned. It was bright and airy. Her kitchen was amazing. The fireplaces turned even the spacious rooms into cozy refuges from the increasingly bitter weather of fall. They had already had one blizzard, and another was predicted before the end of the week. The snow was deep at the higher elevations, but here in Winding River it had melted rapidly, leaving mud and gloom in its wake. It was only the beginning of November, and already she was dreading being closed up indoors with a man who retreated into moody silences more nights than not.

But Cole, despite the fact that he was reluctantly sharing her bed, still kept a part of himself distant. They made love—sometimes sweet, tender love, sometimes wild, passionate love—but there was little joy in it.

Still, Cassie couldn't deny herself the one form of communication that Cole allowed. Nor could she regret what had happened because of it. They were going to have a baby. She'd planned to tell him when he got back from his business trip, though she had no idea how he would take the news.

Once in a long while she caught a glimmer of the old Cole, the man who had shared everything with her, the man who had trusted her with his most private thoughts. Other times it was like living with a stranger. Which, she wondered, would surface when she made her announcement?

A lot depended on that, because slowly but surely their current circumstances were draining the life out of her. She had to do something to fix it, but she was out of ideas. It wasn't possible to force someone to forgive, much less forget. Time, the great healer, wasn't working. And a baby couldn't be expected to save a faltering marriage.

Cole's father was no help at all. He reserved most of his snide comments for the times when the two of them were alone. Cassie usually managed to let them roll off her back. Fighting with Frank Davis was a waste of energy, at least over something as inconsequential as a few pointed remarks.

His attempts to turn Jake against her were something

else entirely. She wasn't sure when she'd first realized that was what he was doing, but lately he'd stepped up the campaign.

Today Frank dropped Jake off at the end of the drive after a riding lesson at the Double D. Jake came into the kitchen with a sullen expression, uttered no greeting at all and started to walk straight past her. The show of belligerence, more and more frequent after he'd been with his grandfather, was the final straw.

"Hey, what's with the long face?" Cassie asked.

His reply was mumbled. He kept right on walking.

"Jake Collins, get back here."

He faced her with a dark look. "I'm not a Collins. I'm a Davis. Someday I'm going to own Grandpa's ranch."

He said it as if he expected her to challenge the claim. "I imagine that's true, if it turns out to be what you want. As for whether you're a Collins or a Davis, you were born with my name. If you'd like to think about legally changing that to Davis, I'll speak to your father."

Having Cole legally acknowledge Jake as his son was something they should have discussed, she realized. In fact, she was somewhat surprised that Cole hadn't insisted on it. Obviously, his failure to do so was grating on his father's nerves. Frank had clearly started planting the seeds in Jake's head to get the ball rolling. Right or wrong, he was manipulating her son, just as he'd tried to do with Cole for years. She didn't like it.

Jake stared at her, clearly surprised by her offer. "You will?"

"Of course."

"Grandpa said you wouldn't. He said you were probably trying to keep me from being a Davis."

Cassie barely resisted the urge to tell Jake precisely what she thought of his grandfather. "That's not true," she said instead, keeping her tone mild. "To be honest, your father and I simply haven't talked about it, but we will. I promise."

Jake studied her intently for a long moment, his expression troubled. "Can I ask you something?"

"Of course."

"Are you and Dad gonna get a divorce?"

Cassie was stunned by the question. "No. Why would you think that?"

"Grandpa said you probably would and then I would live with Dad."

"Oh, he did, did he?" Her temper shot into the stratosphere. If Frank had been around, she might very well have clobbered him over the head with a cast-iron skillet. "Sweetie, your dad and I are working very hard to make us a family. That takes time, but it's what I want. It's what we both want."

"Promise?"

She hugged him tightly. "I promise. Now go on upstairs and do your homework. I need to run out for a little while."

The minute Jake had grabbed a handful of cookies and a glass of milk, she snatched her jacket off a hook by the kitchen door and went to the barn. She saddled up a horse, because it was much faster to get to the Double D by cutting across their adjoining fields than it was to drive clear out to the highway and around.

She had never been quite so furious. Even after learning of the role that Frank and her own mother had played all those years ago in keeping her and Cole apart, she had struggled to understand their perspective, but this was too much. This was an attempt to scare her son, to make it seem as if his family was about to fall apart and that the only person he could rely on was his grandfather.

Her breath turned to steam as she urged the horse into a gallop that ate up the distance to the Double D ranch house. All she could think about was shaking Frank until his teeth rattled. Not that she could do it, given their difference in sizes, but she was darn well willing to give it a try. At the very least, she intended to give him a tongue-lashing that he wouldn't soon forget.

Oblivious to the fact that there were still lingering patches of ice on the ground, that snow had started falling again, she rode harder, her temper climbing.

When the horse lost its footing, she wasn't prepared for the sudden skid, the frantic attempt by her mount to stay afoot. The next thing she knew she was flying through the air, trying desperately to curl her body to protect the baby as the ground rose up to meet her.

But she misjudged. When she slammed into the rocky ground, she broke the fall with her hand and felt the bone snap. The pain was excruciating. And for the first time in her life she fainted.

Cole hated himself for falling in love with Cassie all over again. How could he be so weak that a woman who'd betrayed him not once, but twice, could still manage to steal his heart? He wanted so badly to accept the love she was offering, to move on, but a part of him insisted on fighting her every step of the way.

It had to stop. They couldn't go on like this. It wasn't fair to either of them, nor to Jake.

Cole came home after a two-day business trip to California prepared to let her go so they could both find some peace. He walked into the house to find the kitchen empty with no sign of dinner on the stove. He heard music from upstairs and gathered Jake was in his room doing his homework, though how the kid could think with that sound blaring in his ears was beyond Cole.

He climbed the stairs two at a time, knocked on Jake's door, then opened it without waiting for a response. He doubted his son could hear him over the music, anyway.

Sure enough, Jake didn't even look up from his books. Cole crossed the room and switched off the CD player. Jake blinked and stared at him, his expression brightening.

"You're home. When did you get here?"

"A few minutes ago. Where's your mom?"

"Isn't she downstairs?"

"No."

The response seemed to make Jake vaguely uneasy.

"Jake, what's going on?"

"I'm not sure."

"Did you two fight?"

"Not exactly. I just asked her about some stuff Grandpa said. I think maybe it made her mad. Maybe she went to see him."

"What did Grandpa say?"

"That you guys were gonna get a divorce and I was gonna stay with you. She said he was wrong." Worry puckered his brow. "He was wrong, wasn't he?"

Cole bit back a curse. Given what he'd been thinking when he walked in the door, his father hadn't been that far off—though only about the divorce. Cole didn't intend to try to keep Jake. Now was not the time to get into that, though.

"When was that?" he asked instead.

Jake shrugged. "I don't know. What time is it now?"

"After seven. It's already dark out."

"I guess it was about four. I went by Grandpa's after school for a riding lesson, then he brought me home."

Three hours? Cole thought, his stomach churning. Why on earth wasn't she back by now? He grabbed Jake's phone and called his father.

"Is Cassie there?" he demanded when his father answered.

"Cassie? Why would she be here?"

"Jake thought she might be heading over there."

"Maybe she just wised up and left you."

Cole let that pass. The most important thing right now was finding Cassie.

"I'm going out to look for her," he told his father. "If you give a damn about me or my son, you'll help."

"Well, of course I will," his father said defensively. "The snow's been coming down awhile now. No telling where she might be. Car could have run off the road."

But when Cole went outside, Cassie's car was parked behind the house where it always was. He checked the barn and saw that one of their horses was missing.

He looked up and realized Jake had followed him outside. He was shivering just inside the door of the barn.

"Is she gone?" Jake asked, looking as scared as Cole felt.

"She took one of the horses," he said. "I'm sure

she's fine. She probably took shelter somewhere when the snow started.''

''Why wouldn't she have turned around and come back?'' Jake asked reasonably. ''Or gone on to Grandpa's?''

He hunkered down in front of Jake. ''I don't know, pal. I need you to do something for me, though. I want you to go inside and call nine-one-one. Tell the sheriff we need some help looking for your mom, okay? Can you do that?''

Jake nodded, his eyes wide.

''Then call your grandmother and ask her to come out here and stay with you.''

''I want to come with you,'' Jake protested.

''No, this is more important. You can be the biggest help to your mom by calling the sheriff. Now scoot.''

With one last backward glance, Jake took off for the house. Cole saddled their second horse and rode off in the direction of the Double D. If it had had to snow today, why couldn't it have been earlier so there would be clear hoofprints for him to follow? Instead he was forced to slow down and guess which way she might have gone.

The temperature had dropped dramatically just since he'd gotten home. If Cassie was out here, injured, she wouldn't be able to last long. The sense of urgency doubled, even as his progress slowed.

''Come on, Cassie. Where are you? Help me. Give me some sign.''

The distant, distressed whinny of a horse finally drew his attention. His own mount's ears pricked up.

''Is that Harley?'' he murmured, and got a shake of a head and an answering whinny as a response. ''Find him then. Let's find Harley.''

The terrain had grown rockier and slicker. His frustration mounted right along with his anxiety. He had to find Cassie. He damn well didn't intend to lose her like this.

With a sudden rush of understanding, he realized that he couldn't lose her at all. What did the decision of a scared eighteen-year-old girl matter? If the decision of a twenty-eight-year-old woman was less understandable, even he could see that it had been driven by a fear just as deep-seated as the one she'd felt years before. Who was he to judge that?

All that mattered, all that had ever mattered, was that he loved her and she loved him. Nothing had ever changed that. They'd just lost their way for a while.

Now he had to find her and tell her that.

A heart-wrenching whinny of an animal in pain cut through the air, closer now, just over the rise, if he wasn't mistaken. He crested the hill and spotted them, horse and woman, both down, both way too still.

"Don't die, Cassie," Cole pleaded as he leaped to the ground and knelt beside her. In its own show of concern his horse edged closer to its disabled stable mate. "Dear God, please don't let her die."

He checked her carefully for injuries. The only obvious one was her broken arm, but she'd been here a long time. Could it be there was a more serious problem? He debated the wisdom of moving her, but the chances of anyone else coming upon them here were slim and time was essential. She'd already been out in the bitter cold for way too long.

He bundled her in his jacket, then checked the injured horse. "I'll get someone in here for you in no time," he vowed, running his hand over the horse's trembling flank. "You saved her life, you know. You told me how to find her. I'll do everything in my power to save yours, too.''

Then he gathered Cassie into his arms and mounted his own horse, heading for home as quickly as the weather permitted. She moaned softly while he rode. She was obviously in pain, but she was alive, and for the moment that was all that mattered. Once he got her to a hospital, he would will her back to life.

The next hour was the longest of his entire life as Cassie fought her way back to him. When her eyes finally blinked open, her gaze wandered around until it locked on his.

''I knew you'd find me,'' she whispered hoarsely and then closed her eyes again.

The next time she awoke, Cole was asleep in the chair beside her bed. His eyes snapped open when he felt her fingers against his cheek. Her color was better, her eyes clear.

''How do you feel?''

''Alive,'' she said. ''And grateful. Every time I tried to move, my arm hurt. I kept fainting.''

He sighed when he met her gaze, then did what he'd vowed to do when he thought she might be lost to him forever.

''Good, because I have something to tell you, and I need to do it now, before I lose my courage. If you want your freedom, Cassie, I'll give it to you. Jake will stay with you.''

She stared at him with an expression he couldn't read, so he plunged on.

''I didn't give you a choice about marrying me before, so I'm giving you one now. I love you. I want you to stay, but if you want to go, there will be no custody battle.''

There was no mistaking the sheen of tears in her eyes then, and for an instant he was terrified that his gamble wasn't going to pay off, that she would go.

"You love me?" she said, and there was a note of wonder in her voice.

He shrugged. "Always have. I guess I always will. I just lost sight of that for a time." He studied her intently. "So, Cassie, will you go or stay? You can have some time to think about it."

"I don't need to think about it, not even for a second." A smile blossomed on her face, then spread. "Since I think we're about to have another baby, it looks like I'd better stay." She rested her hand protectively on her stomach. "Now I can't wait to know for sure."

"And if you aren't pregnant, will you still stay?"

"Yes, of course, because I love you and this family of ours. I was just beginning to wonder if you were ever going to figure out that we all belong together. I'd pretty much concluded that the media had gotten it all wrong all these years, that you weren't half as smart as they were always writing."

"I was smart enough to marry you," he said. "And to keep you."

She touched his cheek, her eyes shining. "Love me, Cole. Right here, right now."

He laughed at the urgency in her voice. "Sweetheart, you have a broken arm, bruised ribs. You were half-frozen when I found you."

"Then you can warm me up," she said.

Cole couldn't resist the invitation. He closed the door to the room, then deliberately turned the lock.

Then he nudged her over in the hospital bed until he could sneak in beside her and love her the way she was meant to be loved, with total concentration and finally, at long last, with his whole heart.

Epilogue

"Jennifer Davis, what have you been doing? Rolling around in the mud?"

Cassie stared at her four-year-old daughter with dismay. They were having a party in twenty minutes, and Jenny was covered from head to toe in dirt. It was all over her clothes, even in her hair.

"I've been baking cakes," she announced happily. "For Grandma. See."

Cassie followed the direction of her daughter's gesture and groaned. There were, indeed, a half dozen "cakes" on the backyard table, each with a candle stuck crookedly into the mud. The vinyl tablecloth was a mess.

"I'm sure Grandma will be thrilled," she said. "Now get in here and let's see if we can clean you up."

Jennifer darted through the door and straight into her

daddy's arms. Cole scooped her up before he realized the condition she and her clothes were in.

"Sweet heaven, now you need a bath, too," Cassie said. "What am I going to do? The guests should be here any minute. Mother will be mortified if Dr. Foster finds half of her family looking totally disreputable."

"I don't think your mother's going to be all that worried about a little mud. We're celebrating the fact that she's just gotten a clean bill of health after five years. She's a survivor, Cassie. Nothing else matters." His grin turned wicked. "Besides, I think the doctor is long past being shocked by anything we do. He's been asking her to marry him for the past four years. Clearly he's accepted the whole package."

Cassie still couldn't get over her mother's long-distance courtship with the surgeon in Denver who'd saved her life. It was the happiest she'd seen her mom in years.

Of course, she was still declining his proposal for reasons that eluded all of them. Cassie feared it had something to do with her, though her mother flatly refused to talk about it.

"Take your daughter and get cleaned up," she ordered Cole. "I'll try to scrub up the picnic table. And if you can pry Jake away from his computer, I'd appreciate it."

"Don't spoil my cakes, Mommy," Jenny pleaded, eyes bright with tears. "They're for Grandma."

Cassie sighed and went outside. A few minutes later her mother and Dr. Foster arrived, followed shortly by Frank Davis and the Calamity Janes. No one seemed the slightest bit dismayed by Jenny's contribution to the food, least of all Cassie's mother, who seldom took her gaze away from the doctor, anyway.

"They look blissfully happy, don't they?" Cassie whispered to Cole.

He grinned. "Not as happy as the two of us, but yes, they do look as if they're in love."

"Maybe I should give her a nudge, tell her to marry him."

"She's a grown woman. I'm sure she knows her own mind. Maybe our news will help."

She touched his cheek. "It will certainly reassure her that there are no more bumps in the road for us."

A few minutes later Cole stood and announced a toast. "First to our mom," he said. "You've proved just what a survivor you are."

He turned to Cassie. "And to my wife, who is about to make me a father again. Family and friends are what life is all about, and I can't tell you how grateful we all are to be here together today."

To Cassie's dismay her mother looked shaken by the news of the new baby. And Dr. Foster's expression turned resigned. Cassie crossed the yard and confronted her mother.

"Okay, what is it? You're not sick again, are you?"

"No, of course not," her mother said at once. She glanced at the man beside her. "It's just that we were considering getting married."

"Mom, that's fantastic. I couldn't be happier."

Her mother shook her head. "No, it's not possible. You're having another baby. I have to stay. And what Cole said about family. He's right. We need to be together."

"Now, Edna—" the surgeon began.

"Don't," her mother said sharply, cutting him off. "This is the way it has to be."

Cassie exchanged a look with the doctor.

"Okay," he said finally. "Then I guess we'll just have to go about this another way. I've talked to a few people. I can move my practice to Laramie. I'll be retiring in a few years, anyway, and this will be a good transition. If need be I can go to Denver and consult if something comes up with one of my patients there."

Cassie watched her mother's eyes begin to sparkle.

"You would do that?" Edna said to him. "You would give up your life in Denver?"

He nodded. "I'm a lot like your son-in-law. I know a good woman when I find her, and I'll do whatever it takes to hang on to her."

Cole joined them then, his gaze questioning. "A happy ending?"

Cassie looked up at him and nodded. "For all of us," she whispered. "Definitely a happy ending."

* * * * *

And now, turn the page
for a sneak preview of
ABOUT THAT MAN,

the exciting new novel by
Sherryl Woods

On sale in June 2001
from MIRA Books.

1

Daisy Spencer had always wanted children. She just hadn't expected to wind up stealing one.

Okay, that was a slight exaggeration. She hadn't exactly stolen Tommy Flanagan. The way she saw it, nobody wanted the boy. His father was long gone, and his pitiful, frail mother had had the misfortune to die in the recent flu epidemic. The story was the talk of Trinity Harbor and had been for weeks now.

While they searched for relatives, Social Services had placed Tommy with three different foster families in as many weeks, but Tommy wouldn't stay put. He was scared and angry and about as receptive to love as that vicious old rooster Daisy's father insisted on keeping over at Cedar Hill.

Despite all that, Daisy's heart just about broke when she thought of all the pain that ten-year-old had gone through. She figured she had more than enough love to spare for the little boy who'd been one of her brightest Sunday school students, a boy who was suddenly all alone in the world, a boy who'd lost his faith in God on the day his mother died.

She knew all about tests of faith and enduring tragedy. For months now she had been on the verge of resigning herself to living on the fringes of other people's lives, to being Aunt Daisy once her brothers married and had families of their own. Today, though, everything had changed.

Early this morning she'd gone to the garage and found Tommy, cold and shivering in the spring chill. He'd been wearing a pair of filthy jeans, a sweater that had been claimed from the church thrift shop, even though it was two sizes too big, and a pair of sneakers that were clearly too small for his growing feet. His blond hair was matted beneath a Baltimore Orioles baseball cap, and his freckles seemed to stand out even more than usual against his pale complexion.

Despite the sorry state he was in, he had been scared and defiant and distrustful, but eventually she'd been able to talk him into coming inside where she'd fixed him a breakfast of eggs, bacon, hash browns, grits and toast. He'd devoured it all as if he were half-starved, all the while watching her warily. Only in the last few minutes had he slowed down. He was pushing the last of his eggs around on his plate as if her were fearful of what might happen once he was done.

Studying him, Daisy felt a stirring of excitement for the first time in years. Her prayers had been answered. She felt alive, as if she finally had a mission. Mothering this boy was something she'd been meant to do. And she intended to cling to the sensation with everything in her.

* * *

With each day that passed, Daisy felt more and more confident that she had done the right thing. Tommy was filling her too-quiet house with noise and even now there was the scent of freshly baked chocolate chip cookies in the air.

Still, there was always the chance that this dream world she'd created could come tumbling down around her.

When the doorbell rang, she froze. Wiping her hands on her apron, she took her time answering it. But instead of the social worker who could take Tommy away, or her father who'd been ominously silent on the subject of Tommy, she found her minister, Anna-Louise Walton, on her doorstep. The redheaded pastor had already made a huge difference in town with her blunt talk and warm compassion.

Now, however, when Anna-Louise returned Daisy's welcoming smile with a somber look, the likely implication of this unannounced visit sank in. Apparently King Spencer, Daisy's father, had sent the pastor over to do his dirty work and deliver a lecture on the mistake she was making by taking Tommy in.

"Here on a mission?" Daisy inquired.

"Why would you think that?"

"Am I wrong? Or are you just here to pay a call on one of your flock?"

"Absolutely," Anna-Louise said.

"A preacher shouldn't fib."

A grin spread across the other woman's face. "Okay, I did get a call from your father a few days ago. He seemed to think you required counsel."

"I imagine what he said was that I needed to have my head examined."

Anna-Louise chuckled. "Words to that effect."

"And you agree with him?"

"Actually, I'm on your side on this one."

"You can see that I had no choice, can't you? Tommy needs to have someone in his life he can count on."

"No question about that."

"And I can give him a good home."

"Of course, you can," Anna-Louise agreed.

Daisy's gaze narrowed at all the ready agreement. Despite what she'd said, Anna-Louise wouldn't be here now if Daisy's actions had her full blessing. "But?"

"What happens when he leaves?"

"Who says he's going to? His mother is dead. So is his father. None of the foster families worked out. Where would he go?"

"Frances found his uncle today," Anna-Louise said quietly.

Daisy felt a cry of dismay sneaking up the back of her throat, but she managed to keep it from escaping. She forced a smile. "That's wonderful! Is he coming here?"

"Next Thursday."

"Has he agreed to take Tommy?"

"Not exactly."

Relief flooded through her. "Well, then, we'll just have to wait and see what happens, won't we?"

Anna-Louise put her hand on Daisy's "I know how much you love children. You'd be a terrific mother to Tommy, and you deserve this, Daisy, you really do, but it might not work out. I just want you to be prepared to let go."

"God would not bring Tommy into my life and then

snatch him away. What do you know about this uncle?''

''He's a cop in D.C.''

''Is he married?''

''I don't think so.''

''Then why would he be any better suited to care for Tommy than I am?''

''It isn't a matter of better. It's a question of family. He and Tommy are related.''

Daisy wanted to argue that a loving stranger might be better for Tommy than a bad relative, but until she met this man, she had no right to stand in judgment of him. Anna-Louise would likely tell her she didn't have the right even then. Judgment was God's business.

And so it was, Daisy thought. But just in case He had other things on His mind besides Tommy Flanagan, she intended to look this uncle over very carefully before she relinquished Tommy to his care.

*And now, turn the page
for a sneak preview of*

COURTING THE ENEMY,

*book two in Sherryl Woods's
exciting new miniseries,*

THE CALAMITY JANES

*On sale in August 2001
from Silhouette Special Edition.*

Chapter One

Tears welled up, spilled down Karen's cheeks and splattered on the glossy travel brochures for places she had put off seeing to marry the man of her dreams. A prepaid ticket to anywhere she chose had accompanied the brochures, a gift from her best friends, the Calamity Janes.

They had been wonderful since the death of her husband. Karen loved them all for their support and their generosity. Their hearts were in the right place, but she couldn't see how she could go to Cheyenne for a day trip right now, much less on some dream vacation. The work on the ranch hadn't died with Caleb.

But oh, how she wanted to go. She finally dared to reach for the brochure on London, studied the photos of Buckingham Palace, the Old Vic, Harrods, the cathedrals.

She sighed heavily and reluctantly put the brochure

down again, just as someone knocked at the kitchen door.

When she opened it, her heart thumped unsteadily at the sight of Grady Blackhawk. He'd been at the funeral, too. And he'd called a half-dozen times in the weeks and months since. She'd tried her best to ignore him, but he'd clearly lost patience. Now, here he was on her doorstep.

"Mrs. Hanson," he said with a polite nod and a finger touched to the rim of his black Stetson.

She had the whimsical thought that he was deliberately dressing the part of the bad guy, all in black, but the idea fled at once. There was nothing the least bit whimsical about Grady. He was quiet and intense and mysterious.

"I thought I had made it clear that I have nothing to say to you," she told Grady stiffly, refusing to step aside to admit him. Better to allow the icy air into the house than this man who could disconcert her with a look.

This man, with his jet black hair and fierce black eyes, was now her enemy, too. It was something she'd inherited, right along with a failing ranch.

"I think it would be in both our interests to talk," he said, regarding her with that intense gaze that always disquieted her.

"I doubt that."

He went on anyway. "I've made no secret over the years of the fact that I want this land."

"That's true enough." She regarded him curiously. "Why this land? What is it about this particular ranch that made your father and now you hound the Hansons for years?"

"If you'll allow me to come inside, I'll explain. Perhaps then you won't be so determined to fight me on this.''

Karen's sense of fair play and curiosity warred with her ingrained animosity. Curiosity won. She stepped aside and let him enter.

His intense gaze swept the room, as if taking stock, then landed on the scattered brochures.

''Going somewhere?'' he asked, studying her with surprise. ''I didn't think you had the money to be taking off for Europe.''

''I don't,'' she said tightly, wondering how he knew so much about her finances. Then again, just about everyone knew that she and Caleb had been struggling. ''My friends do. They're encouraging me to take a vacation.''

''Are you considering it?''

''Not with you circling around waiting for me to make a misstep that will cost me the ranch.''

He winced at that. ''I know how your husband felt about me, but I'm not your enemy, Mrs. Hanson. I'm trying to make a fair deal. You have something I want. I have the cash to make your life a whole lot easier. It's as simple as that.''

''There is nothing simple about this, Mr. Blackhawk. My husband loved this ranch. I don't intend to lose it, especially not to the man he considered to be little better than a conniving thief.''

''I certainly don't expect you to just give the land to me, because I say it rightfully belongs to my family. I'll pay you a fair price for it, same as anyone else would. I guarantee it will be far more than what was paid for it all those years ago.''

Before she could stop him, he named an amount that stunned her. It would be enough to pay off all their debts and leave plenty for her to start life over again back in Winding River, where she'd be with friends. It was tempting, more tempting than she'd imagined. Only an image of Caleb's dismay steadied her resolve. Keeping this ranch was the debt she owed to him. She could never turn her back on that.

"I'm not interested in selling," she said with finality.

"Not to me or not to anyone?" Grady asked with an edge to his voice.

"It hardly matters, does it? I won't sell this ranch."

"Because you love it so much?" he asked with a note of total disbelief in his voice.

"Because I can't," she responded quietly.

For a moment he looked taken aback, but not for long. Locking his gaze with hers, he said, "I'll keep coming back, Mrs. Hanson, again and again, until you change your mind or until circumstances force your hand. This place is wearing you down. I can see it." He gestured toward the brochures. "Obviously so can your friends. Make no mistake, I'll own the land, no doubt before the year is out."

His arrogant confidence stirred her temper. "Only if hell freezes over," she said, snatching the back door open and allowing a blast of wintry air into the room as she waited pointedly for him to take the hint and leave.

His gaze never wavered as he plucked his hat off the hook and moved past her. He paused just outside, and a smile tugged at his lips. "Keep a close eye on the weather, Mrs. Hanson. Anything's possible."

Beloved author
Sherryl Woods
is back with a brand-new miniseries

THE CALAMITY JANES

**Five women. Five Dreams.
A lifetime of friendship....**

On Sale May 2001—DO YOU TAKE THIS REBEL?
Silhouette Special Edition

On Sale August 2001—COURTING THE ENEMY
Silhouette Special Edition

On Sale September 2001—TO CATCH A THIEF
Silhouette Special Edition

On Sale October 2001—THE CALAMITY JANES
Silhouette Single Title

On Sale November 2001—WRANGLING THE REDHEAD
Silhouette Special Edition

"Sherryl Woods is an author who writes with
a very special warmth, wit, charm and intelligence."
—*New York Times* bestselling author
Heather Graham Pozzessere

Available at your favorite retail outlet.

Where love comes alive™

Visit Silhouette at www.eHarlequin.com   SSETCJR

SILHOUETTE® MAKES YOU A STAR!

*Look in the back pages of
all June Silhouette series books to find an
exciting new contest with fabulous prizes!
Available exclusively through Silhouette.*

Don't miss it!

Silhouette®

Where love comes alive™

*P.S. Watch for details on how you can meet
your favorite Silhouette author.*

Visit Silhouette at www.eHarlequin.com   STEASE

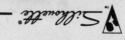

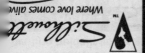

Coming soon from

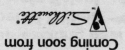
Silhouette™

SPECIAL EDITION™

EXTRA!! The Times EXTRA!!

GINA WILKINS

gives readers the scoop in
her juicy new miniseries

Hot Off
the Press!

Catch the latest titles in 2001

THE STRANGER IN ROOM 205
(SE #1399, June 2001)

BACHELOR COP FINALLY CAUGHT?
(SE #1413, August 2001)

And look for another engaging title
in October 2001

Available at your favorite retail outlet.

Silhouette®™
Where love comes alive™